Prais

THE PALA(

first in t

GW00726015

"Charming and compelling, this magical adventure story will entertain and enchant in equal measure." *Santa Montefiore*

"This is a fantastic adventure - exciting, compelling, clever - with magic, legend and mystery and links back and forth in time to history." *Juno Magazine*

"The Lion, the Witch and the Wardrobe meets Tolkien."

"This book captivated my daughter on the first page. She then read the first five chapters without putting it down. No other book has been able to enthral her so completely. I read it to my other children and they loved it, and what's more, so did I."

"This fusion of magic, adventure and excitement is a breathtaking novel that you can't put down. I read it in about two days."

"This is a real gem of a book which will transport a generation of pre-teens into a wonderfully vivid fantasy world."

"Absolutely loved it ... definitely a page turner ... read it in two sittings."

"Best book I have read this decade. Absolutely fabulous book, written in 3D just like a film. Got my 8 year old to read, which is a miracle. Brilliant!"

"BEST BOOK EVER"

"My son devoured this book ... he's rated it alongside the Morpurgo books which in his eyes are tip-top."

"This is one of those books that you stumble across and are so glad you did. I was thrilled to find a book like this to read to my children. Magic and adventure. What more could you want?"

"I read this cover to cover and couldn't put it down. It transported me into their magical world. My children can't wait for the sequel. They love Tolkien and Potter and we can now add a Loveridge to the list."

"Steven is obviously a very bright and talented author."

"Great!!!!! It was awesome. Everything about it is great. It was so believable and magical. It is one of the best books I have ever read."

"This book is truly amazing. I have been reading it to my children and they love it. They don't want me to stop reading!"

"Effortlessly fusing magic and adventure with time-travelling thrills, The Palace Library will be eagerly pounced on by children who loved Harry Potter or the Chronicles of Narnia. The central characters are likeable resulting in readers genuinely caring about their well-being as they journey through the mythical Tolkien-inspired realm that Loveridge has so elegantly crafted." *Primary Times*

Comments are quoted from reviews on Amazon if not otherwise marked.

Guardians
of
The Scroll

Steven Loveridge

Steven Loveridge

A CIP catalogue record for this book is available from the British Library.

Printed and bound in Great Britain by Clays Ltd, St Ives plc

ISBN: 978-0-9574357-5-9

Leofric Digital
Sandpit
Broadwindsor
Dorset DT8 3RS
United Kingdom

leofricdigital.com

For Mamma

The Palace Library
Series

The Palace Library
Guardians of The Scroll

Contents

1.	The Traitor	11
2.	The Chimney	15
3.	Punishment?	18
4.	The Library Opens	23
5.	Theft Discovered	29
6.	The Broken Lift	35
7.	Trapped	38
8.	Arrest	43
9.	Footprints in History	51
10.	The Slave Girl	58
11.	Ptolemy Neos Philometor	62
12.	Pyrros	69
13.	Fire!	73
14.	Sacred Crocodiles	77
15.	Nicomachus	82
16.	The Battle with the Cat	86
17.	Harry and Neos	95
18.	Ordeal by Hydra	101

19.	A Plan	109
20.	Disguise	115
21.	Swapping the Scroll	121
22.	Recapture	126
23.	Arson	133
24.	Departing for Rome	137
25.	The Archers	143
26.	Fear of Water	147
27.	Escape	151
28.	Underground	160
29.	The Babel Charms	166
30.	Confessions	173
31.	Reconnaissance	179
32.	The City of Rome	184
33.	Kidnap	189
34.	Challenge	194
35.	Cleopatra's Curse	200
36.	Guardians of The Scroll	207

Followed by the first chapter of the sequel.

1. The Traitor

A screech. A thump. The cracking of glass.

Harry was falling in darkness. He couldn't see. He couldn't breathe. He tried to thrash around. He couldn't move. He tried to scream. He couldn't make a sound.

Tap-tap-tap. Tap-tap-tap. Tap-tap-tap.

Harry realised that he was locked in a nightmare. But the tapping wasn't in his dream. It was real, repeating like an alarm clock, battling to wake him.

Harry opened his eyes. He wasn't blind after all. He could see a dragon's claw in his arm, shrouded in smoke. He heard himself scream. The ground was rushing towards him and he was going to be crushed. No. It was water below, dark and murky, waiting to swallow him. He was going to drown. With a desperate struggle, he turned his head and managed to breathe a proper mouthful of air.

His face was in his pillow and his hands were spread out either side of him like a sky-diver. He could move them. He scratched the scar on his arm. It was throbbing gently, but not agony. "It's still just a scar," he said out loud. Hearing the sound of his own voice calmed him. The faint glimmer of light through the curtains felt different to the darkness before. Yes, now he really was awake.

Tap-tap-tap. Tap-tap-tap.

Something was knocking at the window. This was real, not part of the dream. Harry got out of bed, pulling a thin blanket around him to keep warm.

The heavy curtains scraped noisily across the old brass rail as he drew them open. His room looked across the garden towards the great cedar tree and the ha-ha. The windows of the old house were lead-paned in diamond patterns. One pane was broken and ice had drawn feathers of frozen condensation on the inside. No wonder Harry was so cold. Crystals gathered under his fingernails as he scraped frost off the window to see out. Suddenly he jumped and goosebumps crawled up his arms. The beak of a bird thrust forward, tapping at the glass.

Tap-tap-tap. Tap-tap-tap.

Harry fumbled at the latch of the window, stiff with age and ice. He gave it a thump and it suddenly jerked wide open. The bird fell off the windowsill.

"Hell!" muttered Harry to himself. The bird spun and tumbled before recovering near the ground. It swooped back across the roof of the house. "At least it's not hurt," thought Harry as he saw it fly. Its feathers were the colour of tarnished brass. He had the strange feeling that it was trying to tell him something.

Clouds high in the sky drifted across the winter moon as it struggled to light up the garden. A gap in the clouds allowed Harry to see the old cedar tree clearly. To his surprise, he noticed two people standing in its shadow, backs towards him. One was tall, thin, a dark grey hoodie covering his head. The other was shorter, stout, with a long old-fashioned cloak draped over his shoulders. The night was still, so Harry could just about hear what they were saying.

"You're sure this is the genuine thing?" said the tall person

- definitely a man - flicking through pages of paper.

"There's no doubt. It's the most precious artefact in The Palace Library. It's rare, unique probably." The high-pitched voice trembled: "Is it valuable?"

"Yesss," hissed the tall man, drawing his fingers across the pages to feel them as much as read them.

"Then you'll pay me what you said?" asked the other. "Perhaps I should ask for more?" The voice cracked.

Harry stared in disbelief as the tall man moved his hand from the sheaf of papers to the neck of the shorter person and squeezed it tight. "More? More? This was taken from my family a long, long time ago. You ought to have nothing at all." The hand moved away from the short man's neck and he condescended to say, "You shall have what I agreed. That is all."

Harry started to cry out "Stop!" Some instinct held him back, but not before the 'S' echoed round the garden like a hiss. The taller man turned and looked up. Their eyes met for a moment that felt like minutes. Harry threw himself below the window. He was sure the sound of his heart thumping on the floorboards would be heard all over the house. He knew the tall man had seen him. He could still hear the strangers as he lay flat on the bedroom floor, as frozen with fear as he had been in his nightmare.

"Who was that?" demanded the tall man.

"It's just a boy," said the other. "Harry. He often comes to stay here. Don't worry about him."

"Harry? You're sure?"

"Yes. I told you, he comes to stay with his sister, Eleanor. They're just children."

"Don't tell me they have another friend? Grace?" He spat the name out like a bad taste in the mouth.

"Yes, but how do you know?" asked the short one.

"They are trouble."

If Harry had been able to see them, he would have seen the thin hand strike again and squeeze until the other was on his knees. "You will not be paid until they are dealt with. You'll hear from me again soon. Now go. GO!"

Harry heard someone running as fast as they could, panting. And although Harry had not seen the assault, he felt their fear. The short fat person would have seen the same face and be terrified, as Harry was terrified. The tall man had a pale gaunt face, skin taut across the bones, ancient. But it was the eyes that were frightening. Harry had never seen eyes like that. They were demonic. They looked like cat's eyes, alive with orange fire. The pupils were single black needles, filled with hate.

2. The Chimney

Harry cowered on the floor for several minutes before he dared to lift his head. His teeth were chattering. The blanket had fallen from his shoulders and lay crumpled on the floor. Cold air poured in through the open window and wrapped around him, but he was already frozen with fear. He had to shut the window. Now. Without being seen. He stretched out his arm and pulled the metal frame tight and twitched the heavy curtains together. The wound from the dragon's claw ached, even though it had fully healed months before. He rubbed the scar, a habit that had formed without him noticing. He had to get warm. He looked around and spotted a box of matches on the mantelpiece.

Harry wasn't sure if he was allowed to light the fire, but he was so cold he didn't care if he got into trouble with Horrible Hair Bun, Great Uncle Jasper's witch of a housekeeper. He needed to warm up and think. He struck the first match, but the matches were damp and the head just withered away into nothing, dropping a tiny glowing spark on the hearth where a pile of twigs, wood and bark lay ready. The next two matches were the same. Harry took three matches at once, holding them at arm's length, and struck them together towards the centre of the fireplace.

One of the match heads flew back at him. "Damn and blast," he muttered as it burnt the skin on his hand, making him drop the box. Sucking the burn, he threw the spent matches into the centre of the pile of twigs. The glow of the match heads faded into nothing, but a tiny column of smoke began to rise upwards. There was a rustling, and a trickle of dust began to fall down the chimney, followed by chunks of soot mixed with more twigs and moss. Something was bumping around in the chimney. Harry crouched and tried to look up, but leapt back quickly as dust dropped into his eyes. A bird fell with a thump into the centre of the twigs. It flapped a couple of times, coughed and spluttered. It was covered in soot and dirt. So was Harry's face, he could feel grit on his eyeballs.

The bird's eyes were shut. It flapped once or twice more, and then was still. Harry stepped forward, blinking and rubbing his eyes, forgetting the cold. As he bent towards the hearth, he realised it was the same bird that had tapped on the window, but it seemed smaller and withered, grey rather than the colour of tarnished bronze. He thought he should pick it up and take it to Eleanor, who knew what to do with injured animals. Then, as he bent down to pick it up, the twigs in the fire burst into flame, as if they were the head of an enormous match, and the whole pile began to burn furiously.

Instinctively Harry stepped back, and tripped over the edge of a carpet. "Ow!" he yelped as his bottom hit the wooden floor with a thump. The flames engulfed the bird and everything else in the fireplace. Harry wondered how he could help it, looking desperately around for some sort of tool to reach into the fire, but there was nothing.

Sickened that he could do nothing, Harry stared as the fire grew stronger. At first, it was a deep, golden colour, and then, even though the twigs were burned to ash, there was still a fierce green flame. Harry saw something moving within the fire. Was the bird that had come down the chimney still alive? It was! But he couldn't get close. "What can I do?" he shouted in frustration. From green, the flames turned to blue, and then to orange. Suddenly the creature stood up, wings outstretched, fanning the last of the fire into a massive conflagration. It looked as if it was bathing in the flames.

This wasn't the small frail bird that Harry had seen. This was much bigger. This bird was pure, brilliant white with a wingspan that touched the sides of the chimney-breast.

Harry suddenly thought of the blanket. He could wrap it around the bird and smother the flames. However, when he turned back from picking it up, it was too late. The bird's wings were moving so quickly that Harry lost sight of their shape, and their draught extinguished the flames. All that seemed to be left of the fire was burning in the bird's tail-feathers. Piercing sapphire-blue eyes stared at Harry, and he felt that he was staring at a person. Then the bird lifted its wings and flew from the fireplace. The last remnants of flame streamed from its tail feathers in all the colours Harry had seen: red, green, purple, blue and orange. A trail of smoke followed the bird and filled the room. It flew around the bed twice and sat on the mantelpiece, folded its wings and preened itself. The fire in the hearth went out, and the fire on the bird's tail was gone. The room was dark.

Sleeve across his face, spluttering from the smoke, Harry opened the window, trying not to show himself to anyone outside. The bird flew past Harry's head so closely it brushed against his hair, and then went straight up into the sky.

Crouching low, Harry saw it circle and swoop around the top of the cedar tree. Harry dared to raise his head and look around carefully. There was no sign of the people he had seen before, or the terrible eyes. The bird was hovering with its wings outstretched. Harry was sure he heard the bird say, "Thank you."

But he put the thought aside because, of course, birds don't speak.

3. Punishment?

Harry's mind was racing as fast as his teeth were chattering. What on earth was the bird? What were those two people doing in the middle of the night in Great Uncle Jasper's garden? Was this the beginning of some new adventure? Someone had been stealing something, and one of the thieves was hardly normal - hardly human. "Have to get warm to think," he thought. Pulling open a drawer, he dragged two jumpers over the top of his pyjamas, rummaged in a cupboard and put a jacket on top. Then he nearly fell over pulling on a pair of trousers, the pyjamas beneath sticking out ridiculously.

The twigs in the fireplace had burnt so fiercely that nothing remained in the hearth but the tiniest trace of white ash. Looking around, Harry realised that there weren't any logs in the room, so he wouldn't have got far with lighting a fire anyway. Having his clothes on made him just a bit warmer. He decided to get back into bed, but not before grabbing an old cap and a scarf off the back of the door.

Still shivering under the bedclothes, he heard the grandfather clock at the end of the long corridor strike the hour. Only four o'clock! He was desperate to speak to his sister Eleanor and his cousin Grace but there was no way he could creep along the squeaky corridor without waking Horrible Hair Bun. When he

18

had last done that he had been locked in his room for a whole day with nothing to do. He sighed in frustration. It was all too unreal and a reminder of the events last summer that had started here in this big house and The Palace Library.

With these thoughts winding around and around in his head, Harry decided to wait until he heard the six o'clock chimes. He might get away without too much grief from Horrible Hair Bun then. Minutes seemed like hours as he heard the quarters and the hours strike. There was no chance of sleep with so much to think about. But then, to his surprise, once he had warmed up a little, Harry did exactly that.

When he woke, daylight was seeping through the curtains and Harry felt much better, though still not very warm. He was glad he was fully clothed, otherwise he might have thought the whole thing was just part of his nightmare.

He leapt out of bed and ran down the corridor. The grandfather clock's hands stood at twenty-eight minutes past eight. Help! Breakfast was at half-past. Horrible Hair Bun always insisted that they were all at the table by then, otherwise they would go without. Harry pelted down two flights of stairs to join the others in the kitchen and sat in his place just as the clock chimed the half-hour. Horrible Hair Bun scowled at him as she set down a plate of eggs and bacon. Whatever else was wrong with her, her cooking was good.

"I'm so sorry. I nearly overslept," he said politely. It made no difference to her scowl.

"Take your cap off. It's ridiculous to wear it inside." When Harry did so, she scowled again, "Wash your face properly after breakfast."

"Just in time, Harry," said Eleanor, winking at him.

"How do you wink like that?" asked Grace, scrunching her

eyes in an unsuccessful attempt to copy her elder cousin. Then she saw Harry and giggled. "What are you wearing? You look like a fat scarecrow!"

"Never mind. I need to talk to you both," whispered Harry.

He gobbled his food, barely chewing the bacon. He couldn't wait till Horrible Hair Bun left the kitchen. She always went to check their rooms, eager to scold the children if they were too untidy. Harry hadn't made his bed, so he knew he'd be in trouble, but he was more anxious to tell the girls about the bird, the fire and the strangers. As soon as Hair Bun had left the room, he started talking excitedly.

"Slow down Harry!" said Eleanor. "You look as if you're about to explode. And finish chewing first! You're spraying toast crumbs all over me. It's disgusting."

Harry gulped so quickly at a glass of water that some of it dribbled down his jumper. "This is serious," he began.

As he finished telling his story Grace looked at him out of her clear blue eyes and said, "Are you sure you didn't set the little bird on fire, Harry?"

"Of course I wouldn't have set the bird on fire! I didn't even know it was there. And anyway, I barely managed to get a spark off the matches, let alone set the twigs on fire."

"There's a boy at school who does horrible things to animals," said Grace. Harry frowned and Grace suddenly realised that it sounded like an accusation. "But I know you're not like that. I was just checking."

"You mean the fire just started by itself?" asked Eleanor.

"I know it sounds strange," said Harry, still cross from Grace's accusation but having the sense to ignore it. "The fire just erupted on its own. The matches wouldn't work. And anyway I've never seen a fire that burned so quickly or fiercely."

"I wish I'd been there to see it," said Eleanor. "The thing I don't understand is why the bird was white." Harry was about to ask what did that matter, when he realised what he had missed. Stupid! he thought. Maybe the cold had got to his brain in the night.

"I thought they were…" said Eleanor, but Harry interrupted, "It's a Phoenix. Of course!"

"Durr," said Eleanor. "Of course it's a Phoenix. It was being reborn in your fireplace and you didn't even realise? Durr."

Grace, who hadn't realised either, decided not to own up but changed the subject instead, "What about the people? Who were they?"

"The tall man - if he was human at all - I'm sure I've never seen before."

"Then how did he know you?" said Grace.

"I dunno. It's weird."

But then there came the familiar screech of Horrible Hair Bun in a temper.

"Here it comes. We're in trouble now," said Harry.

"You're in trouble, you mean," replied Eleanor.

Horrible Hair Bun threw open the door and looked at Harry, finger pointing. He froze, bracing himself against the torrent of words he was expecting about not making his bed. But they didn't come at first. As Harry and the girls looked at Horrible Hair Bun, they saw her draw her breath in, before bellowing in a louder scream than ever before, "Harry Godwinson. I have to say, I never expected it of you, especially at your age. I will not have you smoking in this house - or at all."

Harry looked up. "I wasn't smoking!"

"Don't try to deny it!" screeched the housekeeper. "I can smell the smoke quite clearly in your room. And you've broken a window."

"Harry wouldn't smoke," interrupted Eleanor. "Not after his experience last summer. He's telling the truth!"

"'His experience last summer?' You mean to say that Harry has been smoking before? It sounds as if he wasn't punished enough."

"That's not what I meant," said Eleanor, twisting a loose strand of hair, realising she had made things even worse.

"Well, Harry," asked Horrible Hair Bun. "Did you smoke last summer?"

He stammered, "It … It's a long story, and it's not really mine to tell."

"A simple yes or no will do."

"Well, yes. But I had to."

"That's absurd," said the housekeeper.

This time Grace spoke out, "You're not being fair! Harry was just trying to light the fire in his bedroom. Can't you see he's frozen? And then the matches didn't work. He couldn't even light the kindling wood. He told us."

Horrible Hair Bun was silent for a moment, but only a moment. "I've had enough of you covering up for Harry. There hasn't been a fire laid in that fireplace in my lifetime. The chimney has always been blocked up. Aha, I've caught you now, haven't I? I'm going to take you to see your Great Uncle Jasper right now. He will know what to do with you and he will decide how to punish you, Harry, for smoking and all of you for lying. I expect he will beat you."

4. The Library Opens

Horrible Hair Bun frogmarched the children across bare oak floorboards to Great Uncle Jasper's study. Ancient portraits of men wearing beards and old-fashioned clothes looked down at them sternly as she knocked at the door.

"Enter."

Horrible Hair Bun threw open the door. Warmth and cosiness wafted out of the room before the children even stepped inside. A pile of well-read books wobbled and then settled back into organised chaos. A fire crackled between two huge sets of bookshelves. Strange artefacts with unknown uses filled gaps in various places on the shelves.

"Are you cold, Harry?" asked Great Uncle Jasper from behind a big mahogany and leather desk. For the first time that morning, Harry became self-conscious about what he was wearing. He still had his school scarf wrapped around his neck and was holding the old tweed cap in his hand.

Before Harry had a chance to answer, Great Uncle Jasper asked, "Which room is Harry sleeping in?"

"The green room in the West Wing," Horrible Hair Bun said.

"I think we'd better move him. The fireplace doesn't work there and the chimney is blocked up. It must be terribly cold with all this frost. I'll keep the children here for the moment till Harry has warmed up."

"I've brought them here for punishment."

"Oh?" Great Uncle Jasper's eyebrows lifted high up his forehead.

"Harry has been smoking and these others covering up for him."

"Has he indeed?" The eyebrows dropped into a frown.

"In his bedroom."

"That sounds most unwise. Stupid even - so easily discovered. Leave the children now. I'll deal with it. I've some other things to discuss with them, as it happens." He looked at the children with a stern face before turning back to the housekeeper. "Perhaps you could organise Harry's bedroom now?"

Horrible Hair Bun looked disappointed, as if she didn't want to miss out on any punishment the children might be getting. "Shall I wait here in case you need me, sir?"

"No, thank you, Mrs. Higgsbottom. I will look after this myself."

After the housekeeper left the room Great Uncle Jasper pulled open a drawer of his desk and took out a small brown package wrapped with string. He put it down in front of him, tapping it with his fingers.

"Sit down, children. Sit down."

The girls sat on the cushioned fender in front of the fire, but Harry, beginning to overheat in so many layers, sank into the little armchair opposite the desk. Great Uncle Jasper knew, of course, about Harry's adventures the previous summer, which the housekeeper did not. He frowned and for a moment Harry became more worried. Great Uncle Jasper seemed to be a kind man, but none of the children knew him well.

He looked at Harry and said, "It would surprise me if you have been smoking after your experience at Hell's Bay last summer Harry. Were you?"

"No, sir."

"Well that's that, then," said Great Uncle Jasper.

"You believe me?" asked Harry.

"Of course. You don't strike me as the lying type. None of you do," he added, looking at the girls.

"But I don't understand how the bird could have fallen down the chimney if the fireplace is blocked up. All I was trying to do was set light to all the twigs in the hearth," said Harry.

Great Uncle Jasper raised his eyebrows again. "I think you had better explain more about the bird. Make yourself comfortable and tell me your story. Perhaps you might start from the beginning - always a good plan. " His eyes twinkled as he added, "After all, Mrs Higgsbottom might never forgive me if I didn't ask you. She does seem to become stricter with time." So Harry told his tale for the second time that morning. As he talked, from time to time Great Uncle Jasper tapped his fingers on the little parcel, especially when he heard about the stranger with the fiery eyes. When he had finished, Great Uncle Jasper said, "You're sure both these people knew about you, but you couldn't recognise them."

"Yes. Quite sure. They were too far away. But those eyes. I'll never forget them. They were horrid - like demons. The other funny thing is that the bird seemed to be trying to tell me something, some message, but I don't know what. He wasn't talking exactly. I know it sounds silly, but it was more like a voice in my head, in a language I couldn't understand."

"That is odd," said Grace. "Maybe it's a bit like Sophie, and her empathy."

25

"Yes," Eleanor added, "And I bet Sophie thinks so too. Don't you, Sophie?" She turned to the noble deerhound lying on the Persian carpet in front of the fireplace. While Harry was telling his story, Sophie had silently crept up and pushed her nose into Eleanor's hand. Eleanor was stroking her.

"Well, well," said Great Uncle Jasper. "That's another surprise this morning, but at least it's not an unpleasant surprise. Tell me, Eleanor, where did Sophie come from?"

"Wh - what do you mean?" said Eleanor, nervously, as if she'd done something wrong. "She was just here all of sudden. I supposed she'd been here all along."

"No," said Great Uncle Jasper. "Don't you recall? Sophie lives in The Palace Library. She shouldn't be here at all. She should be with Edgar and Eloise. This can mean only one thing. The Palace Library and this house must have become linked again."

"So that's how the Phoenix came to fall down the chimney," said Grace.

"Perhaps," said Great Uncle Jasper, deep in thought. "Without doubt you seem to have seen the rebirth of a Phoenix. You are privileged. Very few people in the whole history of the world have seen it. There is only one Phoenix and he is reborn in fire every few hundred years. No one knows when it will happen. I have never heard of the Phoenix ever being any colour other than gold, except in heraldry and there's a connection with The Palace Library there too. This is curious."

"I suppose it was a bit gold when I first saw it at the window and falling down the chimney, but it was so sooty. When it came back to life it was definitely white," said Harry, still too shaken by the whole experience to really consider it a privilege.

Just then a voice boomed through the wall behind Great Uncle Jasper, and said, "It's not quite right that the Phoenix is always gold, but another colour is very unusual. A White Phoenix is recorded in Plutarch's Life of Caesar. That's apart from the one on the Council of the Book's heraldic shield. Could you give me a hand, do you think?"

"Edgar!" shouted the children happily, recognising the voice.

Behind Jasper, one of the piles of books on the floor had begun swaying from side to side. The top few books slipped off the stack and hit the floor. A large and heavy bookcase nearby began to wobble.

"I think something's blocking the door," shouted Edgar. The bookcase began to wobble more dangerously.

"Wait!" commanded Great Uncle Jasper. "Girls, clear these books out of the way. Quickly. Harry, help me move the bookcase."

Harry and Jasper both grunted as they pushed the heavy bookcase. Behind it was a simple wooden door, without a handle.

"Try now, Edgar," said Jasper.

"That's better," said the voice on the other side and a moment later the elderly man who had befriended the children the year before stood before them, unchanged with his silver-grey beard and deep blue tail-coat covered with gold brocade. As he tried to stand up straight, the children mobbed him. He mustered all the dignity he could to greet Great Uncle Jasper with formality, "Good morning, Sir."

"Good morning, Edgar."

Edgar said, "I think you'd better come in. When Sophie vanished and the magical door appeared, we hoped we might see you. Eloise has gone to make some hot chocolate. The food's improved no end since she's taken an interest in the cookery section. The hot chocolate's from a Belgian book, I think.

27

They're masters of chocolate, you know, the Belgians."

The children looked round at their Great Uncle. "Go on," he said kindly. "That's an offer we can't refuse. Once we're in the Library, we can try and get to the bottom of these thieves as that is what they seem to be - and of The Phoenix."

"Just watch out," said Edgar, "This door has appeared in a most unusual place. The geography of the place is all muddled up."

5. Theft Discovered

Sophie leapt through the door, but the last thing she expected was a highly polished mahogany table on the other side, slippery as ice. She did the splits with her front feet and her nose whacked the table. Her hind paws had no better grip and she slid over the edge on her tummy, tumbling to the floor with a yelp.

"Sophie!" cried Eleanor, nearly falling herself in her anxiety for the dog, but by the time she was through the door Sophie had picked herself up. She shook herself and stood up. elegant once more, smiling in her own way.

"It's a map table," announced Edgar, making his way much more gingerly. "I really don't know what right a door has to be on top of a map table. A door should be in a wall."

Grace walked cautiously to the edge. Then she saw Eloise beneath her, holding her arms up ready to catch her. The intention was clear but Eloise said nothing. She couldn't. She was mute. With a huge smile Grace launched herself into her arms.

Eloise's long dark hair was tied back in a plait and she wore a plain dress. She looked completely different from the forlorn prisoner she had been at the end of their adventures the previous summer. At that time she had had a shaved head and had been dressed in rags. Now even the scar that disfigured half her face seemed to fade as she smiled in obvious pleasure at seeing them all.

A set of library ladders stood at the edge of the table and Edgar climbed down. Harry turned back to look into Great Uncle Jasper's study and stared at the mess of books on the floor. "I think Mrs Higgsbottom will have something to say about this when she sees it. I do hope she won't blame you, Harry," said Great Uncle Jasper. "Carry on. I'll join you in a moment."

Harry jumped down from the table and Great Uncle Jasper turned back into his study. He collected the small brown package wrapped with string and slipped it into his pocket. As his foot touched the floor of The Palace Library, there was a loud bang. The door slammed shut. The whole quivering frame now sank into the table, which began to shake like a jelly. Within seconds, it vanished without trace.

As if all this had been the most normal thing in the world, Great Uncle Jasper said politely, "Good morning, Eloise." She curtsied to him and nodded her head. Then she turned to the children and smilingly indicated the hot chocolate waiting for them.

The grown-ups had small, delicate porcelain cups, with a swirl of dark chocolate inside them. The children had steaming mugs with a milky frothy top. Dragons flew round and round in circles on Harry's mug. Grace's was dark blue with twinkling stars. One of the deerhounds running around Eleanor's mug was just like Sophie.

"Can I have some marshmallows, please?" asked Grace with her most angelic smile. Eloise frowned.

"She doesn't know what marshmallows are," said Edgar. Eloise had come to the Library from her own time of 1164 and still had a lot of catching up to do. "They're a sort of sweet, Eloise. You should find a book on the second shelf behind you."

Eloise found the book, turned to the page on marshmallows

and showed Grace the picture. "Yes please!" said Grace. So Eloise tipped the book and the marshmallows fell right off the page into the cup. "Wow! Thank you."

While all three of them had a portion of marshmallows Great Uncle Jasper told Eloise and Edgar about the Phoenix and the strange people stealing something.

"I think this morning's events justify these three knowing more, don't you, Edgar?" said Great Uncle Jasper. "More to the point, I think they need to know now, without further reference to the Council."

"Well, that was my advice to the Council last year, but it was not taken," replied Edgar a little pointedly.

"I know, Edgar and you know I agree with you."

"Non maior sed sanior," muttered Edgar.

"Come on, Edgar, you know the Council takes a vote. We can't overrule it just because we think we're in the right. That's the route to dictatorship and what we strive to avoid. I may be head of the Council, but I cannot ride roughshod over what everyone thinks."

"I know, I know."

"What does, er, what you said, mean?" asked Harry. "It's Latin, isn't it?"

"It means 'Not the most, but the wisest,'" said Jasper. "Dictators use the principle to overthrow a majority vote - and freedom. A principle of 'I know best', if you like. Anyway, it's time to tell you more about the Council. In the circumstances, could you find a copy of the heraldic arms of the council, please Edgar? Do you agree?"

"I agree."

"In fact, I think it's time they saw Katherine's book."

Edgar hesitated. He thought for a moment or two, then said,

31

"Yes. I agree with that too. Democracy in action, you see," he said to the children. He grinned at Jasper. "I won't be long."

Edgar tottered off to find the book. When he returned, his face had not just gone white, but ashen grey. He put down a large leather-bound volume on the map table as if it were a great burden, then staggered and held onto the table with both hands, breathing hard. "It's gone! Vandalised, stolen! We have failed!"

He slumped, and might have collapsed if Jasper had not caught him. Edgar managed to stand up more firmly and flung open the leather book. His gnarled hands took a chunk of pages from within and flung them into the air. They settled like leaves on the floor around him. "Look. There's nothing but blanks in the binding. It's been taken. Cut and vandalised! Stolen! Replaced with blanks! On our watch!"

The demonstration seemed to be his last effort. As he finally collapsed into a chair, head in his hands, he said, "I have failed," over and over again. Then he looked up at Jasper, pulling himself together, and said, "The Council must be called at once. This is the most serious thing since the fire."

Jasper nodded. He looked pale and shocked, but unlike Edgar, he didn't seem to be panicking.

"What's missing? What fire?" asked Eleanor.

"The book was almost lost in the Great Fire of London in 1667, but that's another story. Before that, it was in its original form - a scroll. Only after the damage from the fire was it bound up in a book."

"Maybe it's what I saw being stolen. There were certainly papers," said Harry.

Great Uncle Jasper sat down and took a deep breath. "We cannot know for sure, but yes, I think you're right. We must do whatever we can - whatever - to recover it."

"How old is it exactly?"

"We don't actually know." Jasper paused, grasping the remains of the book in his hands. "Very soon, we must convene the Council of the Book, the group which for hundreds, even thousands of years, has protected it. But you need to know more. Without doubt, you are heavily involved in this, more so perhaps than even we ever imagined." Edgar was nodding, silent. The hot chocolate was forgotten.

Great Uncle Jasper opened the vandalised volume. Only the title page remained. It was a brightly painted picture of a coat of arms, but instead of a conventional shield, it was shaped like a gold-coloured book and at the centre a large white bird.

"That's it!" said Harry. "That's the exact bird I saw this morning!"

"And this," said Jasper, "is the symbol of the Council of the Book. It was drawn when the book was rebound after the fire, but the symbol of the White Phoenix is important and his actual arrival just now ... well, can it really be a coincidence? The missing pages are important too. They're the pages we've come to know as Katherine's Book."

"So who was Katherine?" asked Grace.

"Katherine was a member of the Council of the Book at the time of King Arthur, but, from the little we know, she was old, possibly mad, and shunned by the Court. Merlin believed what she said, however, and persuaded King Arthur to take her under his protection."

"But aren't King Arthur and Merlin just stories?" asked Grace.

"Like we thought dragons were just stories until last summer?" said Harry, rubbing the wound on his arm.

"Exactly, Harry." said Jasper.

"And the Scroll, the book thingy?" asked Eleanor. "What can

be so important about one book? Is it just because it's old?"

"No, no. Not just that. In the wrong hands, that book is one of the most dangerous things in the world."

"More dangerous than bombs and missiles?" asked Grace.

"Much more dangerous," replied Great Uncle Jasper. "The Scroll is just one part of a much larger Scroll. Katherine told Merlin and Arthur that, combined with the other parts, it could be used to wake, control or destroy all the powerful creatures of The Nether World, the creatures - or monsters - who lurk under the surface of our world. It can be used for both good and evil, which is why it must be protected."

"The Council of the Book is sworn to protect this book and look after it. We have failed," Edgar added dismally.

"Then we need to recover it," said Harry. He thought back to the previous summer when the children had been sent to fight dragons in the past. Was this happening again?

"Let me tell you more," continued Jasper.

"Hush!" said Grace. "Listen!"

Jasper looked quite startled to be interrupted like this by Grace, but he listened for a moment.

Tap-tap-tap. Tap-tap-tap.

"That's what I heard in my nightmare, but it turned out real," said Harry.

Tap-tap-tap. Tap-tap-tap.

"It's the Phoenix. He wants to come in. He's at the window on the gallery by the dome." Grace stood up and pointed. "He's got a message to give us."

"How do you know?"

"I just know. And I know it's urgent." Without another word, she ran to the stairs and began to climb them two at a time.

6. The Broken Lift

Harry and Eleanor looked at each other in mutual understanding. "We'll go after her." They remembered the long flights of stairs from their last visit to the Library. Edgar was hardly going to argue, nor was Jasper. The Palace Library soared above them and they could see the circular gallery. Above that was the great dome.

They began to climb. As they went up, Harry remembered the way the backs of his knees had begun to ache only a quarter of the way up the one hundred and twenty-seven steps. His knees were beginning to ache now. He envied Eleanor, climbing steadily. At least they could come back down in the extraordinary lift they'd used once before.

"125, 126, 127," said Harry and Eleanor together finally.

"Come on!" shouted Grace. The Phoenix was tapping at a window on the other side of the gallery around the dome. A balustrade with a narrow stone top ran the whole way round in a circle - and Grace ran along the top of it, careless of the drop.

"Watch out! You'll fall!" shouted Harry.

"'Course I won't," said Grace, showing off. Peering over the balustrade, Harry could see the long, long drop to the ground floor. Just staring at it made him feel sick. He knew he wouldn't have the balance to do it and he could hardly watch Grace as he and Eleanor raced to the other side on the much safer gallery floor.

Harry began to drag a chair over to the window to reach the latch, but even then Grace beat them to it. She jumped from the balustrade and climbed up the bookshelves like a monkey. The window stuck, but they managed to get it open and the Phoenix flew in. It turned and hovered in the air with its wings outstretched. They could have sworn it took a bow before turning and flying down to the ground floor in a graceful spiral.

Grace was so nimble that she was back on the balustrade running the full circle and heading down the stairs again before the other two had even started to move. Her voice echoed around the dome, "I'll be down before you!"

"Come on. This way. Let's take the lift. It'll be quicker. We can beat her," said Eleanor, pulling at Harry's arm.

They had been in it once before with Edgar. It was no ordinary lift. It was more like a fairground ride: a platform that dropped from the level of the dome to the basement and then bounced on a spring until it came to a standstill. Edgar hated it, saying it made his stomach turn. The children loved it.

The Phoenix landed on the map table, beating all the children to the ground floor. In a single cheeky move, it picked at the marshmallows left in Grace's cup and swallowed them whole.

Grace crouched panting, her hands on her knees, and looked at the Phoenix. Its blue eyes sparkled, and they understood each other. "So this is empathy," thought Grace. She could understand what it was feeling. 'It's here to tell us something," she said to Edgar and Great Uncle Jasper, "but it can't remember exactly what it is."

"Rebirth has robbed it of many memories from its past life," said Jasper. "We must be patient."

But then, through the Phoenix, Grace knew something unexpected and frightening had happened. The Phoenix soared back up to the roof and they saw it swoop behind the book stacks, where the lift started. Grace turned pale.

Eloise saw the change in Grace and put her arm round her. "What's wrong?" asked Great Uncle Jasper.

"I don't know," Grace said. "Something's happened to the others. The Phoenix has gone down the lift-shaft." As she spoke the bird swooped up from the basement.

"He must have flown all the way down the lift-shaft and back," said Edgar.

The bird hovered in front of Grace.

"Come on," she said. "We need to get to the basement." The basement was where the lift finished. There were no stops on the way down.

Within minutes, they all stood staring at the bottom of the lift-shaft.

"There's nothing here," said Jasper, bemused.

"Nothing at all," added Edgar.

"What do you mean? They didn't use the lift in the end?" asked Grace hopefully. "Maybe they're coming down the stairs after all?"

"No," said Jasper. "They did use the lift. We heard it start. The platform, the springs, the whole mechanism should be here. It's gone."

"There's only one answer," said Edgar, "They've gone out of the library through another magical door."

"Where have they gone?" asked Grace. "Where?"

"That's the problem," said Edgar. "I have absolutely no idea. There's never been a door at the bottom of the lift-shaft before. They've just gone. Vanished."

7. Trapped

Minutes before, Harry and Eleanor had stood on the mahogany platform of the lift.

"Do you remember how different this is to those modern lifts in London?" asked Harry.

"That skyscraper lift was so smooth," replied Eleanor. "I thought it would make me sick, but I hardly felt it."

"This one might make us both sick," Harry said with a grin remembering the first time they had used it. It was more like a fairground ride, partly magical and beautifully made. With both hands, they grabbed the polished brass handrails, cold to touch.

"Ready?" asked Eleanor.

"Ready."

She took one hand off the rail and pushed a brass lever next to her. The platform dropped away below their feet. It fell so fast they thought it might leave them floating like astronauts.

They held their breath, waiting for the combination of springs and magic at the bottom. It would make the landing more like being on a bouncy castle than in a lift.

Harry and Eleanor both felt uneasy about just how quickly the platform fell. Perhaps their memories were faulty. The lift was not stopping. In fact it was speeding up. The smooth masonry walls either side of the platform gave way to rough stone. They gripped the brass railings tightly, too scared to let go. When they glanced at each other, they only saw fear and cheeks hollowed out from the speed of the wind flowing by. Then they were pitched into darkness and damp cold. Even though they couldn't see anything, they both shut their eyes tight.

To Harry, it felt like his nightmare was repeating. He was falling and blind. But this time there was no doubt. It was real. Had it been some sort of premonition?

Seconds, which felt like minutes, passed. Then a searing heat came like someone opening an oven door. And the light was back. Bright sunlight. But now, opening their eyes gave them no comfort whatsoever. They were in the sky falling at great speed toward a city. The noise of the wind rushed past them, matched only by the sound of their own involuntary screams. The lift platform never slowed.

The ground came rapidly towards them and they braced themselves for the crash.

Then once again they were sinking underground. Then silence. They stopped without feeling a bump. In the dim green light around them they saw the lift break up. The mahogany platform and the brass rails fractured silently into a thousand pieces - and vanished. They were just standing still - no bouncing, no effect of any impact. Their knuckles were white with a grip on rails that were no longer there. They were standing in a small chamber.

Eleanor flung herself at Harry, wrapping her arms around him, "Where are we? Are we still in the Library?"

"I dunno." Even in his confusion, Harry was surprised enough by his sister's hug to be self-conscious. He drew back and looked at her in the dim light. Then Eleanor's eyes widened and she stared.

"What are you staring at?"

"What are you wearing?"

Harry fingered his neck. The scarf he had put on to keep warm was gone. He looked down at himself. He was wearing a long white cotton robe that nearly touched the ground.

"Yuk," he said. "I'm wearing a dress!" Then he looked at Eleanor, "And it's just like yours. I need some proper trousers."

"You're wearing a necklace too," said Eleanor. "Actually, so am I." She pulled a silver chain from around her neck. Harry did the same, and they looked at the small silver cylinders hanging from the chains. They were identical, with a line around the middle and embossed with beautiful markings.

"I wonder what they're for," said Harry. Unimpressed with the girly necklace, he tucked it back under the gown.

"How are we going to get out of her?" asked Eleanor.

Harry rubbed his left arm absentmindedly and began to look around the chamber. It was a square stone room, with plain walls and not much else. They were inside a large cube without doors.

"The light is coming from something luminous on the walls. I don't think we can be in The Library anymore." He spoke out loud, partly speaking to Eleanor and partly to himself. He found it reassuring to think things through, but Eleanor said, "I'm frightened, Harry."

"Yeah," muttered Harry. He was frightened too, but it wouldn't help to admit it. "I think we left The Library when the lift didn't stop at the bottom of the shaft. Or maybe when we came out into that bright sunlight. That's when we arrived wherever we are."

"Or whenever," said Eleanor. Magic and time travel were no strangers to either of them after the previous summer.

"That's true," said Harry.

"But why are we here?"

"I don't know. Stop talking for a moment."

"Why?" said Eleanor.

"Quiet!"

They stood still for a few moments.

"There's nothing at all. No noise. No background rumbles. No animals. Nothing. Odd, isn't it?" His voice echoed around the walls, which whispered the words back at him.

They listened again and still heard nothing. Harry hazarded a guess. "I think we're underground, far away from anything."

"How will we get out?" Eleanor's voice rose. Harry knew she was close to panic.

Then to their huge relief they both heard steps. People walking. Walking down stairs towards them - but where was the door?

Eleanor saw a glimmer of different light and dragged Harry into a corner. He had the sense not to cry out as the harsh grip of her hand twisted his wrist. A hidden stone doorway pivoted on its centre and let pale flickering light into the room. Two people entered the chamber. Harry and Eleanor pressed themselves tightly against the wall in a vain hope that it would make them less visible. Was it possible they could remain hidden? And what was this small room?

The two adults stood with their backs to the children. The man was clothed in a deep purple robe. It was loose fitting and the luminous light twinkled from gold embroidery round the edge. Harry realised that it was a toga. A Roman toga. He could see a white tunic underneath it. The man was quite tall, strong-looking, with hair cut short. Harry could see he was going bald on top.

The other person was a woman, far younger than the man. She wore a plain white garment that fell almost to her feet. There was a gold belt around her slim waist. Gold snake bracelets wound round each of her upper arms, and as she turned her head toward her companion, Harry could see that she was not only beautiful but she must be some sort of queen, for she wore a gold circlet on her black hair. There was a gold snake on her crown, a cobra with hood outspread. Both the man and the woman had such presence that the children felt like shameful intruders, witnessing the private moments of powerful people.

As the door closed behind them, another began to open. Sure of themselves and their privacy, the couple did not turn. The queen placed her hand on the man's arm.

"This is your moment, Caesar. You will become immortal in history. Even greater than Alexander," she said. The man turned his head and smiled at her. Then they walked through the door and down another flight of stairs. The new door began to close.

Eleanor was desperately passing her hands across the wall behind them, looking for the first door.

"It must be here. It must open!"

It was there. But it was too heavy for Eleanor to open on her own.

"Come on, Harry! Push! Let's get out of here!" They pushed, but suddenly Harry stopped and turned round, looking at the door across the room, slowly closing.

"What are you doing?" hissed Eleanor.

"We must be here for a reason," said Harry. "That's why the Library sent us here. That's Julius Caesar. He's a hero, a great Roman general. Come on. We're going to follow them." Harry dashed through the shrinking gap. He looked back. Eleanor had not moved.

"Eleanor! Now!"

She slipped through after him, whispering, "You're mad!" The door shut silently behind them. They heard voices at the bottom of more steps, as well as the sounds of their own hearts beating.

Eleanor pushed back on the door behind them. But it wouldn't budge.

They were trapped.

8. Arrest

Eleanor was shaking. Not from cold or fear, but from anger. She was furious with Harry for bringing them into this vast vaulted room. And she was even more furious that she couldn't lash out and shout at him for being such a fool. She clenched and unclenched her fists as once again she pressed herself against the wall. Things were made worse by a regular drip of water on her neck, snaking down her back.

Harry was unaware of Eleanor's fury. He was excited. Here he was in the same room as Julius Caesar! He'd always rather liked what he'd heard of the great Roman general. He also had a pretty good guess at who the woman was. If he was right, he knew where - and when - they were. He looked around this new chamber.

Two other people were in attendance. Fortunately, they were all stooping over a strange table in the centre of the room. The luminous green light from the walls was stronger here and two giant flares drew yellow patterns on the floor and walls. Incense from the flames tickled the children's throats. Harry was desperate to hear the conversation.

"Is this genuine, soothsayer? You have been here studying it." Caesar's profile showed his famous hooked nose as he spoke to a squat little man, also dressed in a Roman toga. It was far less ornate; plain white edged in purple. "I don't want to be fobbed off with something that's just full of pretty pictures, even if I do decide to use it."

"This is the real thing, Caesar," was the reply.

Harry and Eleanor could glimpse the object they were talking about. It was a scroll. Partially unwound, it lay on top of a table that looked more like an altar. Could it be related to the papers he'd had seen stolen that morning? wondered Harry. Caesar reached out to touch it and the fourth person in the room, a tall thin man wearing a simple unbleached tunic, put his hand out to prevent him.

"Would you touch Caesar? Would you dare?" Caesar said icily, flicking the arm away like a fly.

The thin man bowed low, casting his eyes to the floor. "Forgive me, my lord. The Scroll is ancient and fragile."

"Be assured - it is the real Scroll, my lord and my love," intervened the lady. "It was discovered in the East by Alexander the Great and my forefather Ptolemy. A caste of priests hid it and have guarded it in secret here in his tomb ever since. I, Cleopatra, Queen of Kings in Egypt, learnt of this. Now this Scroll belongs to us. It is my gift to us, together."

"Venal priests and soothsayers are not unheard of in Rome; the people are fooled every day by forgeries in the market," said Caesar.

"We are not the people! And there is no need to bring Alexandria down to the levels of the worst of Rome. Trust me." She was almost purring now, soothing his temper, looking at him affectionately. "You have not begun to explore the mysteries, the magic and the power of Egypt. The knowledge in this Scroll will set us apart from all other rulers before us. Your skills as a general, together with this Scroll, will unite Rome, Egypt and the whole world under our command. Our power will be limitless when we have the creatures of The Nether World at our side."

"My armies will be victorious without your magic," replied Caesar. "We will win in any case. I have no need of the Scroll. It is only my regard for you, my lady, that has brought me here."

"But that wretched half-brother of mine, that treacherous usurper of power, will be using magic to fight against us," Cleopatra replied. "He has access to lesser scrolls. He will have no hesitation in summoning the creatures of The Nether World against us. It is only this master Scroll, the one Scroll that contains all the secrets, that can protect us."

Caesar looked down his hooked nose. "You are wrong," he boasted. "I have the best men. They are perfectly trained. They have the best weapons. Military might will win!"

"You are so stubborn!" said Cleopatra in her soft voice. "Won't you let me help you a little bit?" She took his hand in hers and stroked his cheek.

"Have no fear. I will save your kingdom, my lady," replied Caesar, gazing into her eyes. "This book is indeed a great discovery. Yet this priest says he cannot read it; that no one knows the language. We must set our best scholars on it to work out what it means. It will return to Rome with us."

"If that is your wish," replied Cleopatra with a sigh of satisfaction.

"Only our mortality can then restrain us," said Caesar proudly, "but soon we will have an heir and when he is born, he will build on our work."

"For the ancients, even immortality was a goal. Perhaps that too can be within our reach," said Cleopatra.

"The ancient Pharaohs may have sought immortality," laughed Caesar, "but even they found themselves no better preserved than the mummies in their pyramids. Trust to our own future and to heredity, rather than some desire to live forever."

"Perhaps," she whispered, "Perhaps."

Harry was right. It was Cleopatra! That meant they were in ancient Egypt - in Alexandria, over two thousand years before the talk in The Palace Library that morning. Harry wondered if he would have a chance to meet the two famous people. What would he say? With these thoughts racing, he almost forgot that they were trapped and hiding.

His thoughts were interrupted by a sharp pain in his arm. Eleanor was pinching him, far harder than necessary, he thought, though it was true that at any moment the adults in the centre of the room might turn and see them. They had to have somewhere to hide.

Eleanor pointed upwards and Harry looked up into the towering vault. It was conical, like the inside of a witch's hat. High above they could just make out a tiny circle of light, with dark shapes flitting around. Bats!

Eleanor pinched him again and he shook his arm out of her grip. She was pointing upward again. As well as the bats, there was another shape, a much large bird circling. It was the Phoenix. This bird wore bright golden plumage. It was telling them something, bringing them comfort perhaps? They needed it. Harry looked around for a hiding-place, but apart from Alexander's tomb in the middle, the room was empty.

Eleanor's eyes were focused on the Phoenix. As Caesar and Cleopatra looked more closely at the writing on the Scroll, Eleanor saw the bird dive down the vault and rush towards them. She nearly gasped out loud. Was it going to give them away?

The bird had chosen his moment well. The people at the table hadn't noticed it yet. The bird swept underneath the steps that the children were standing on and then perched at their feet. It pecked Eleanor's ankle lightly before it flew under the steps again. She understood now. There was a gap under the steps, a hiding place, but how could they get there unnoticed?

The Phoenix helped them. It crossed the room and flew low under the faces of the four at the table. Its wings scraped across the surface of the Scroll as it went. Then it hovered in front of the group to draw their attention. At that moment, the two children scrambled into the cavity underneath the stairs and sat still, trying not to gasp. As soon as they were hidden, the bird twisted and flew straight up the centre of the room like a rocket, departing through the tiny round hole in the ceiling.

"What omen was that, soothsayer? And what bird?" asked Caesar.

It was not the soothsayer who answered, but the thin priest, who exclaimed, "The Phoenix!"

"The mythical Phoenix?" said the soothsayer doubtfully.

"Yes. Not seen here since the funeral of Alexander the Great in this very spot, his tomb, hundreds of years ago. Its golden plumage is unique."

"This is a most extraordinary omen, Caesar," said the soothsayer, seeing a chance to impress his master. "It shines glory on your missions and plans. Not only that, the Phoenix is an immortal being, from the very beginning of time. This is an omen that goes deep. It is a symbol of immortality."

Cleopatra gave the soothsayer a searching look and he squirmed under her gaze. "Such words are easy to say, but are they true?" She turned to the thin priest. "What do you think, priest? You are the last remaining of your caste, the one who brought us here to see this Scroll when all others refused. What does this mean?"

The priest bowed. "The Phoenix appears at times of change. His presence is a sign that there is a moment of crisis, of domination and a change in the balance of power in the world. His presence is indeed a powerful omen, Madam."

"You speak too cryptically. You work for me now, not your former sect. What are you saying?"

"Those with honesty in their heart can never live in fear in the presence of the Phoenix."

"You sound like a politician, not a priest," said Cleopatra.

"Hah!" said Caesar, turning away from the Scroll. "What he says rings true for me. I do not doubt the confidence of my own ambition. Come, my Queen. We have work to do."

"I leave the Scroll in your charge," said Cleopatra to the priest, "until Caesar wishes to embark for Rome. You will accompany us when that day comes."

The priest bowed low again. He and the soothsayer took the flaming torches from their stands and followed the two leaders towards the steps. Harry and Eleanor cowered beneath. Each tread echoed in their ears, threatening discovery. Incense and smoke wafted around the children.

As they crouched, inhaling incense, Harry desperately needed to sneeze. He held his nose tight, hoping he had smothered the sneeze. Then, as they heard the stone door closing above them, the sneeze returned. He tried to bury the sound by putting his arm over his nose, but still the sneeze roared like thunder in the silent room. Eleanor angrily dug him in the ribs, but they both stayed silent.

They sat there for minutes. During all this time, without realising it, their eyes adapted to the darkness, since the room was now only illuminated by the distant light of the small hole at the top of the vault and the strange luminous glow from the walls.

Harry sat tight, anxious not to provoke a further reaction from his sister. At last Eleanor moved. He followed her to stand in front of Alexander's tomb.

"Sorry about the sneeze. I couldn't help it."

"You're an idiot," whispered Eleanor. "Not just the sneeze! Getting us trapped here at all! Idiot!"

"Don't you realise who they were?" said Harry. "Caesar and Cleopatra!"

"So? We're trapped, idiot!"

"It's not a table at all," whispered Harry, deciding to ignore her. "It's a sarcophagus! Alexander the Great's in there!"

"Don't be gross," snapped Eleanor, although she realised he was probably right. She looked at the Scroll on top of the table. There were pictures and hieroglyphs, strange images that looked like a type of writing. She began to forget her temper. She was fascinated by the picture on the visible part of the Scroll. "Look, it's some sort of sea serpent."

Harry ran his hand down the symbols from top to bottom and started reading:

"Beware the spell to raise this beast;
None control the Hydra except the Hydra.
Destroy it not with a simple sword;
Three heads will rise from one."

Eleanor interrupted him. "Harry," she whispered, still afraid they were being overheard, "how can we read this? We shouldn't be able to read these symbols." She started on the next sentence in the Scroll, using a finger to read from right to left. "Cau-ter-ize," she began. "I don't know what this means, but I know what it says."

Then another voice made both the children jump.

"Cauterize! It means 'to burn'. As you will if you don't do

49

exactly as you're told." Caesar stood towering above them. Cleopatra was just behind him. "I told you someone sneezed," she said. "Now perhaps you'll listen to me a little more carefully!"

"Humph! Guards! Seize these children, these magicians. But don't damage them. Not yet."

9. Footprints in History

While Harry and Eleanor were being taken prisoner in ancient Egypt, Grace sat slumped in a huge armchair underneath the dome of The Palace Library. She sat still, quite unlike her normal fidgety self, her hands across her eyes, hiding tears that silently slipped down her face. Sophie's large grey muzzle rested on Grace's lap, trying to give comfort, but Grace shrank into herself, unable to accept that her cousins Harry and Eleanor had simply disappeared. Above them, the White Phoenix flew in large circles around the inside of the gallery.

"I wonder if he wants to be let out?" asked Edgar looking up at the ceiling.

"No," said Grace, wiping the tears from her face with the back of her hand. "He's thinking."

"Thinking?"

"He's exercising his wings too. They're new to him."

"How do you know?" asked Jasper.

"I just know," said Grace sharply. She covered her eyes again, then said "I'm sorry I snapped at you." She paused, then went on, "It's as if he's in my head, talking to me when he wants to. I can sort of talk back. But it's not actually talking. There aren't any words. It's a sort of silent understanding. I can't explain it."

"She has the gift of communication, probably a magical gift, handed down in her breeding," said Edgar in his pompous way. He was a little calmer now.

"What do you mean, a magical gift? And breeding? You make me sound like a Christmas present or a circus animal! What about Harry and Eleanor? Where are they?"

"We can't tell. The magic of this Library is hard to fathom. Its power comes from the ancient past and we can't always interpret it. The only thing we can be certain of is that the door was opened for a purpose. Harry and Eleanor - and you, I'm sure - have an important role."

"What if the door opened in the wrong place?" Tears were rising in Grace's eyes again. "You said doors were opening where they shouldn't be. They might be anywhere! You seem to have lived forever. Why don't you know the answer?"

"I haven't exactly lived for ever," said Edgar mildly. "Nor am I immortal and I don't have a 'gift' like you. I was given a potion, a potion far older than anyone can remember. I age slowly, but even now," he smiled, "I am heading for old age."

"So you think I have a magical ability to communicate?" asked Grace.

Edgar was nodding, but Jasper replied this time, "I don't know. That could be the magic of the Phoenix, not you. But you, Harry and Eleanor do have one gift you already know about."

Grace looked up, surprised.

"You have the gift of time travel. What's more, it is a gift no one else has - except Sophie here. We don't think last year was the only time you went back to the past. As you grow up, there will be more occasions."

Grace remembered when they had travelled to 1164 through The Palace Library the previous summer. "But how do you know about this?"

"We know because you have left footprints in history. There are indications in the past that at certain times of crisis there have been three children, but the records are all sketchy. We're only just beginning to learn more about it since your journey last summer. Perhaps the past is where Eleanor and Harry are now."

"It sounds crazy," said Grace. But as she said it, she remembered how crazy their last adventure had been. Would nothing be normal in her life anymore?

"There's more we should tell you," said Jasper, glancing at Edgar. "You need to know about the Council of the Book."

The last thing Grace wanted now was a history lesson. She needed to be doing something to help. It was all so frustrating. She fidgeted, knowing it was a bad habit, but she couldn't be bothered to stop herself. What did it matter now? Then the Phoenix swooped down. At the same time, Sophie barked.

Grace could feel the Phoenix speaking to her and stood up shouting, "There's a new door somewhere! Maybe that will take us to Harry and Eleanor."

The Phoenix flapped his wings, impatient to guide them.

"Come on. Let's go!" said Grace.

"Doors in this library never stay open for long," said Edgar, forgetting his weariness.

"The bag, Edgar. Don't forget the bag," said Jasper.

"Of course." He stooped to open a cupboard, but found Eloise was there before him. She pulled out a scruffy canvas rucksack and slung it over her shoulder, then they followed the Phoenix. Tall mahogany double doors opened out from the domed Library into a room as tall as a church with an arched wooden ceiling and wooden book stacks jutting into the centre.

Grace could see ladders leading to balconies up the side of the bookshelves. Another time she would have loved to climb them. Each ladder would let you reach a few shelves before another ladder took you to the next level. High above them, the ceiling was so convincingly painted with clouds and sky that for a moment she thought there was no roof. They followed the Phoenix, who suddenly descended through the floor, vanishing into nothing. As they caught up, Grace saw that there was a staircase let into the floor. She was the only one of them who didn't have to stoop in the basement passageway at the bottom. Soon the natural light gave way to a strange glow, a natural phosphorescence, greenish in colour. Books lined the walls. But the Phoenix kept moving. There was no time to look.

Natural light crept in from a window high above them in circular space with a much taller ceiling. It was a room like a cross-roads. A great stone font stood in the middle, full of water. The Phoenix stood on the edge, sipping at it.

"Which way now?" asked Edgar, trying to catch his breath. "Three passageways beckon us."

Grace ran around the font ahead of them all, looking down each passageway. "Here! It must be this way!"

"How can you tell? I can only see the dark passage," asked Edgar, staring down the corridor.

Grace saw something different. Bright sunlight shone into the passage, although none of the light penetrated back into the library itself. Outside, she saw a huge square, paved with gold-coloured stone. There was not a car in sight. To the left and right several great columns ran along a colonnade.

Sophie gave a low growl and put her paw up against the opening. The effect was like throwing a stone on a still pond. Ripples rebounded outwards, never bouncing back from the side of the walls. They went on and on until they faded away.

"It's here," said Grace, turning to the others. "Can't you see?"

They all shook their heads and Eloise came up to her side.

"Do you think I have to go through?" asked Grace.

Eloise nodded.

"Can you come too?" But Grace already knew the answer to that before Eloise could shake her head. Eloise could not see through the door, and anyway she could never leave the Library again. The year before she had entered the Library as an outlaw. That had saved her life, but the price was to stay there forever, like Edgar.

Eloise handed Grace the canvas bag she had been carrying, and Grace was about to step through the opening when Great Uncle Jasper said "Wait!" He reached into his pocket and pulled out the small parcel he had brought from his study. He handed it to Grace. "Take this with you. Give it to Harry - maybe you'll need it."

"What's it for?" Grace began, but Edgar said "Hurry, the door won't stay open for long", so she put the parcel in the canvas bag and went up to the opening. The Phoenix swept low over their heads. To Edgar, Jasper and Eloise it just vanished, but Grace and Sophie could see the bird fly out into the Square and high into the sky.

The tramp of soldiers' feet echoed in Grace's ears through the magical doorway. She wondered if she could be seen. Should she hide? But there was nowhere to go, so she stayed where she was.

Two soldiers marched right past the opening into the Library. Roman soldiers. Then two magnificent people came into sight. A man in purple and a tall dark-haired woman. Then more soldiers, armour squeaking against leather, spears held upright.

Two more soldiers brought up the rear, their spears pointing at the backs of two children.

"Harry, Eleanor!" shouted Grace, unable to restrain herself. But they could not hear her through the doorway. Only a large cat-like creature on the colonnade noticed anything. Not a friendly tabby cat, but a tall arrogant feline the size of a cheetah. Patterns of brown and blood-red stripes on its body changed as it walked. Startled by Grace's shout, it began to sniff along the opening. Sophie growled. In response it arched its back and spat towards the doorway, but the spit bounced back into its face, gathering in its whiskers. The cat took a step back and Grace nearly laughed at the surprised expression on its face. With a flick of its paw to clean its whiskers, the cat gave up its exploration and cantered down the steps, taking up a position next to the tall woman.

Grace watched the group hesitantly as they marched across the square. Surely they hadn't seen her? If she moved now the soldiers might catch her, but she might never find Harry and Eleanor again. She made her decision, squeezed Eloise's hand and stepped through the opening.

She was unprepared for the searing heat of the place and the awful smell that made her put her hand over her nose. The long mournful 'caw-caw' of vultures gorging themselves on a dead carcass of something in the corner of the square explained the revolting stench.

The group in the square stopped and Grace wondered if they had heard her, but they were pointing the other way, watching something. Grace slipped behind one of the columns while the White Phoenix flew slowly back across the square. For a moment the vultures were silent, forgetting their greed. The Phoenix flew so close to the top of the Roman General's head that he had to duck and then it swooped behind him and flew on. Grace saw its wings brush each of their heads as it flew between Harry and Eleanor, but it didn't stop. It came straight back to the colonnade.

The woman in the square bent down to pet the cat. She whispered to it and Grace saw the cat sprint after the Phoenix in response.

Then Grace heard the Phoenix talking to her in her head. "I should not be here. The laws of time do not allow it. There is only ever one Phoenix, but he knows. Good luck."

It flew back to the Library and Grace saw it disappear through the opening. Then she almost screamed. The big cat had raced up the steps after the Phoenix and leapt right through the opening as well. Grace could see it come face to face with Sophie. The animals snarled at each other and as Sophie leapt to seize it, the cat made a dash for the door. The magical ripples of the doorway flowed outwards as it made its escape. Sophie's teeth snapped but all she could capture were a few hairs of its tail.

"Go now," Great Uncle Jasper said to Sophie. "Look after them."

10. The Slave Girl

Grace had no idea what to do as she watched Harry and Eleanor being marched along, hands tied behind them and the cruel spears inches from their backs. How could she rescue them, alone and vulnerable? As if for inspiration she looked back at the magical door to the Library and to her joy she saw Sophie creep through the opening.

"Sophie," whispered Grace, "Here!" She did not say it like a command to a normal dog. It was a direction given to an equal. In the shadow of the colonnade, the Royal dog that once belonged to Henry II of England and his Queen in another time and another place, trotted on silent pads to Grace's insecure hiding place. The smell of the vultures and the heavy air was far stronger to Sophie than it had been to Grace. She lifted her nose and sneezed.

"Sh!" hissed Grace. She was afraid to move in case she was captured like Harry and Eleanor, but she knew they must get away from there. They could be seen by anyone coming around the corner. At least she was in the same place as Harry and Eleanor now, but she didn't know how to help them. "Sophie, what shall we do?"

Sophie nudged Grace, urging her to stand up, and they slipped quietly around the corner of the colonnade. Here was a market square. But it was hardly bustling. Cloth awnings that had once shaded merchants and traders flapped raggedly from their poles. Only a few traders had any goods at all. Bickering shoppers fought to capture their attention. A strong smell of spices wafted across on the wind, along with a cocktail of all sorts of other smells, not all of them pleasant.

Grace crept around the edge of the square. As an orphan and only child, she was used to being on her own, and knew how to be quiet and unnoticed. Then she slipped into a smaller square, no bigger than a courtyard, where a big palm-tree provided some shade. All the windows in the buildings around the square were tightly shuttered. No one was around to notice them, and Grace sighed with relief. She and Sophie sat down under the tree. But the relief was only temporary. She was still no nearer rescuing Harry and Eleanor, and now she didn't even know where they were. She put her head in her hands, very close to tears. Then she remembered the canvas bag. At least that was something to do. She could check what was inside.

She found Eleanor's dagger and Harry's chain mail coat and left them in the bag. Digging around in the bottom, she felt something round. It was her watch, hanging from a chain like an old-fashioned gold pocket watch, except this one had a compass on the reverse side. As she put the chain round her neck, she found another chain there already, from which hung a small silver cylinder embossed with strange markings. She saw the line around the middle and realised it was a join. She pulled at it, but nothing happened. She tried twisting it. The two halves fell apart and something fell out. It was a tiny piece of stiff paper, rolled into a neat cylinder. Grace carefully unrolled the paper, but it was blank.

"Uh? What do I do with this?"

59

Then she remembered Harry's magic book from the previous summer. They'd had to ask it questions before anything happened.

"What are you for?" Grace asked the paper.

It worked! Words appeared on the page. At the same time strange symbols appeared, glimmering beneath the words. They were familiar to Grace from something she'd been shown at school.

"What does that mean?"

Again, more words and symbols. Grace stared at the paper.

"Who are you talking to?" said a voice behind her.

Grace nearly jumped out of her skin. She leapt up and turned, dropping the piece of paper.

There was a girl there, about her own height, with black hair tied in a pony tail and deep brown eyes. She wore a smart cotton tunic. The girl said something else but Grace couldn't understand a word. The girl bent to the floor and picked up the piece of paper. Grace snatched it out of her hand.

"Give that back to me!"

"I was going to," the girl said, smiling. "Is it important? It's a piece of papyrus, isn't it?"

Grace was looking at the paper in her hand. This time she could understand what the other girl said. As she spoke, the strange symbols appeared on the paper, with English words underneath. Suddenly Grace understood. The paper was translating the words as they were spoken, but the two girls could hear and understand each other as well. The paper needed to be in contact with Grace. Remembering lessons from last term at school, Grace knew what the symbols were. They were hieroglyphs, the writing of Ancient Egypt. She was in Ancient Egypt.

Grace rolled up the paper and quickly put it back into the necklace. The other girl was still standing there smiling. Grace liked the look of her.

"So who were you talking to?" the girl asked.

"I was just talking to myself. I do that sometimes." Grace said truthfully.

"I do too when I'm on my own. I guess it helps me feel less lonely," said the other girl.

Grace decided to be friendly. "I'm Grace." She held her hand out to shake the other's hand. The other girl stared at it. Obviously she didn't know what to do. Then she held her own hand out. As Grace shook it, the other girl's face lit up with another smile. "I'm Katerina, but nearly everyone calls me Kasya. My mother's the head slave in Queen Cleopatra's household. Where do you come from? You've got a beautiful dog."

Grace had heard of Cleopatra, the fascinating ruler of Egypt, but she had learnt the previous summer to be careful about revealing where - or rather when - she was from. She talked about Sophie instead.

"She's lovely!" said Kasya. 'May I stroke her?'

As she bent forward to touch Sophie's head her sleeve fell back from her arm and Grace saw a nasty red mark on it, blistered and sore.

"How did you do that? It looks nasty."

Kasya quickly drew her sleeve down to cover the mark. She hesitated and was about to speak when a deeper, husky voice answered from behind them.

11. Ptolemy Neos Philometor

Grace jumped. She hadn't heard anyone coming. But what about Sophie? Why hadn't she growled or warned her? She was surprised to see that the dog looked vacant, dazed as if in a daydream, but still sitting up. Kasya stood there, rigid, staring at the ground, and Grace saw the girl was trembling. She turned to look. The deep-voiced person was just a boy. Older than her, for sure. Older than Harry too, but still a boy, not tall either.

The boy said, "It's a burn, isn't it, Kasya?"

Kasya didn't answer.

"You can speak now. You have my permission."

"Yes, sir," said Kasya. "It's just a burn." But from the way she said it, Grace knew it wasn't true. She looked directly at the boy's eyes. They were dark brown, but there didn't appear to be any light in them. The iris, the black centre of the eye, merged straight into its brown surround.

Ignoring Grace, the boy waved Kasya away. "Run along now. I am sure your mother will need you." Kasya hesitated. "Now, I said!" Kasya ran off without any more explanation, and without a goodbye.

Even though the sun was burning on her back, Grace felt a chill run through her at that moment.

The boy spoke again, smiling, as if his character had changed altogether or a spell had been broken. His bad temper vanished and the sun shone on his face.

"Well it's clear you are no slave girl, or you would not dare to look at me like that. It would be disrespectful." Though he smiled, his tone was serious. "But I don't know you. Where are you from? Are you a traveller trapped by the siege?"

Grace hadn't worked out what to answer, so she bent and fondled Sophie's head. The dog shook herself, as if summoned from a deep sleep. Only then did she notice the boy and gave a deep low growl.

"That's funny," said Grace. "It was as if the dog was asleep, sitting still with her eyes open, till I touched her."

The boy laughed insincerely. He didn't try to befriend the dog as Kasya had, in spite of saying, "He's a beautiful dog. I haven't seen one like this before. You're a stranger to Alexandria, aren't you?"

Grace nearly asked him where Alexandria was, but realised how stupid that would sound. Instead, she corrected him. "Sophie is a she, not a he. She belonged to a Queen and she's with me now."

"Stolen, is she?" the boy asked, but like a partner in crime, rather than an accuser.

"No! She's not stolen. She's her own person. She doesn't belong to anyone."

"Not like Kasya then," said the boy. "She's a slave and she belongs to my mother. My mother can do what she likes with her. So can I."

Grace did not like the way the conversation was going, but since this was the son of Cleopatra, she did not want to be rude. She bit her lip, trying to think. "I wonder," she said, looking up at the boy angelically, "whether you might be able to help me?

You see, I travelled here with my family, but I've lost them. Can you help?"

The boy didn't reply. He stared, as if he were probing her mind. Grace wasn't quite sure what to make of it. The stare was just long enough to be disturbing. Then the boy shook himself, as if he was waking himself up. He smiled again, and again his personality changed, as if a light had been switched on in a dark room.

"I'm sorry," he said. "You must think me really rude to stare. It's just that I've never seen anyone with blue eyes like yours before."

His words and his smile were disarming. Grace was inclined to give him a second chance and said, "I think all my family and most of the people I know have blue eyes."

"Really? What is your name?"

"I'm Grace," she said simply, uncertain how to deal with his sudden change of character. She didn't offer her hand to shake this time.

"My name is Ptolemy Neos Philometor, but you can call me Neos," he said. "Let's go back to my Palace. There are bound to be people who can help you there. Follow me. You can bring the dog."

Grace followed him, carefully noting where she had been and where she was heading. Sophie was with her, close to her side, head straight and proud, nose high, breathing in all the smells as she went. It was as if her daze when she first saw Neos had given her a heightened awareness.

Piles of rotting rubbish in the streets assailed Grace's nose. A fresh whiff of salty air was a relief and she was about to ask where the sea was when she realised how much that would betray her ignorance.

They criss-crossed some alleyways and Neos took her past a huge, closely guarded gate. "We could go in there, but I'm going to take you my secret way into the Palace. The guards just snitch my whereabouts to my mother all the time. And there are so many of them at the moment. Not that they'd dare touch me. No one else knows about this, so don't give me away."

Grace felt pleased to be part of Neos's secret, but she wondered whether it was done deliberately, to make her like him. She looked up at the walls, sentries standing guard high above. Past the gate and round a corner now, the huge walls of the main Palace rose on their left.

"There's a storm drain here at the bottom of the wall," said Neos. "I discovered it years ago, but you have to be small to squeeze under. The wall's about four feet wide. Wriggle through it on your tummy."

Grace looked nervously at the tiny arch at the base of the huge wall and wondered if this was really such a good idea. Sophie sniffed inquisitively at her side, nose down to the arch.

"You go first," said Neos. "I'll keep watch so nobody sees us. Go on then!" he added, impatiently.

The deerhound took the lead and wriggled her way into the gap like a terrier after a rabbit. Her wagging tail stirred up a mini dust storm until it vanished. Grace dropped down commando-style to follow, pushing her bag ahead of her. The sharp stink of the drain, fortunately dry at this time of year, rose up under her nose. Grace was aware of the terrible weight of the walls above and what would happen if they crushed her. She struggled forward to the faint light ahead of her. Her head popped out of the gap and she stood up, breathing deeply. Sophie was shaking dust off her coat. Leaves and white flowers were all around them. They seemed to have come out in the midst of a bush, or vine, its scent sweet and flowery after the stink of the drain. Neos was behind her so quickly that she hardly had time to take her bearings.

"It's a jasmine plant. Stinks doesn't it?" whispered Neos. "It's really handy, as even if the garden slaves are here, they won't see us. Not that slaves would dare talk to me or turn their eyes to me," he added arrogantly.

They slipped through a garden gate. "We're all right now," Neos whispered. "We're allowed here."

As they turned the corner, his voice changed. "Damn! Wretched people! I'd forgotten they'd be here now."

A crowd of people, mothers with skinny babies in their arms, children in rags, were all waiting by a doorway in a large building. Some of the women stretched their hands, some tried to push to the front, but most stood quiet. At the edge of the crowd were soldiers with big spears - the Roman pilum - watching, waiting for trouble.

"They're allowed to come for scraps from the Palace kitchen at this time of day. Then, thank heavens, they're driven out into the streets. Filthy beggars!"

Neos began to push his way through the edge of the crowd, thrusting with his arms. But the people were not interested in him; when they did see him they stepped aside. His smart clothes were a contrast to their rags.

As he pushed through, the crowd began to surge forward. The door had opened and there to Grace's surprise stood Kasya with men and women carrying baskets full of bread and other scraps. When Grace turned to look for Neos she saw that he'd reached the other side of the crowd. He saw Grace and beckoned her, but the crowd had made him angry. His eyes had changed, the pupils narrow like a cat's. Fire seemed to flicker in their dark depths. Grace remembered Harry's description of the old man he had seen in the garden - was it only that morning? "Like cat's eyes, burning with fire" he'd said. Was that the connection that had brought them here?

She saw Kasya beckon urgently. Her eyes were pleading - but not just pleading, they were offering sanctuary. Grace moved towards the door as the last of the baskets were put down on the ground. Kasya dragged her through. As the door slammed behind them, she could hear the crowds rushing towards the baskets, desperate for food.

Kasya hugged Grace tightly as if she were a long-lost friend. "Thank goodness I got you away from him. You mustn't trust him. He has a way of fooling people into thinking he is nice. Come in." She turned to lead the way. Grace grabbed at her arm as she turned, wanting to ask more. Kasya winced and pulled away.

"Oh, I'm sorry, Kasya! What did I do?"

This time Kasya pulled up the sleeve of her tunic. Her arm was sore and blistered from the wrist to the elbow.

"It's him! It's a burn he did deliberately." There were tears in Kasya's eyes. "He tortures me like he tortures animals. I can't do anything. I'm a slave - lowest of the low - and he knows it."

"You poor thing. It's not your fault," said Grace.

"But he makes me think it is! He is so charming - you've probably seen that now - and then he preys on you. I hate him! And the siege is just making him worse."

"It's really not your fault. But tell me about this siege? What's going on?" said Grace.

It was enough to stop Kasya's tears in surprise, "What's going on?" Then she looked into Grace's blue eyes and asked, "Where are you from? I knew you were a stranger when I first saw you.

But who are you?"

Grace looked back at her. She had had doubts about trusting Neos but she realised she had no doubts about trusting Kasya. And she needed a friend. "Can you keep a secret?"

Kasya nodded.

"First," said Grace, "I need a hiding-place."

Kasya nodded again.

There was a deafening sound, followed by a moment of absolute silence. Grace's ears were ringing. Then she heard words shouted from sentry to sentry, like an echo, "Fire! Fire! The harbour is on fire!"

12. Pyrros

Harry and Eleanor had been marched along by the guards and put into a small square cell. They were locked up and left alone. There was nothing to sit - or sleep - on except for two stone plinths jutting from the walls, without mattresses or even a straw covering. A tiny grating near the ceiling was a poor second best to a window. Eleanor made straight for a small spot near the corner where the sun struggled through the grating. Harry went to sit next to her. The warm sunlight might cheer him up too.

"Don't you dare sit here!" Eleanor shouted. "This is all your fault!"

"How can you say that!"

"You got us trapped in that spooky tomb. You sneezed. It's perfectly obvious it's your fault. If I'd had anything to do with it, we'd have gone up those stairs and we would never have been caught."

"Don't be stupid!" said Harry. "The guards would have caught us just the same. We'd have never have seen the Scroll or the Phoenix in that square. And we'd never have known where we are or where the Library had sent us."

"Well, I wish I'd never even heard of The Palace Library," shouted Eleanor. She turned her head away and wouldn't look at him.

Harry didn't admit it, but he was inclined to agree with Eleanor's feelings about The Palace Library, not that they had any choice in the matter. The Palace Library was choosing them. Harry knew his sister well enough to know she was in no mood to listen to reason. Was it only a few hours ago that they had been safe in the Library, drinking hot chocolate? And where was Grace?

The crash of guards standing to attention, the unbolting of the door, and a brief command cut short their thoughts. With an imperious gesture to the guards to stand away from her, Cleopatra swept into their cell.

She was not really beautiful, thought Eleanor, though she moved with sinuous grace, like the cat that came into the room with her. Her nose was too large and her dark eyes were too penetrating. But there was something fascinating about the Queen. It was hard to take your eyes off her. As she looked them over Eleanor felt Cleopatra was reading her mind. Both children instinctively stood up.

Beside Cleopatra stood the cat that had been with her in the square and chased the Phoenix. It was large, something like a cheetah, but its colouring was different. It moved into the light and she could see the marking more clearly. Its chest and front paws were striped like a tiger, but the stripes were blood-red and dark brown, like the shading of a desert. Yet the animal's hindquarters, still in the shade, were shadowy grey, the same colour as the stone floor. The cat sat down in front of Eleanor, now fully in the sun, and the hindquarters changed to the blood-red tiger stripes. The cat began to groom itself.

"So you like my cat?" asked Cleopatra.

"Yes."

"Is that how you address a Living Goddess, Queen of Kings,

70

The Mistress of Perfection?"

"No, er, Your Majesty," stammered Eleanor, uncertain how to reply to such weird titles.

The Queen smiled, satisfied. "You may stroke the cat."

Eleanor reached out and put her hand on its head. Immediately the animal opened its jaws and the sound it made was no purr, but a roar of fury. Eleanor could see right down its throat. She could also see that its two incisor teeth were curved sabres, like those of a prehistoric cat, but retractable, unseen when the cat's mouth was closed. Fire burned within its eyes, split only by a pinprick of black pupil in the centre. With a single claw, the cat scratched Eleanor's arm from her elbow to her wrist. The burning pain made her cry out, but the skin was not broken. Eleanor snatched her arm away and jumped back into the corner with a shriek.

Harry leapt forward, forgetting his earlier tiff with Eleanor, but Cleopatra took hold of his hair and held him back. "Enough, Pyrros!" she said, laughing. Her voice was cruel, quite different to the one she had used before. "The cat will not hurt you. Not unless I command it." The voice became soothing again. "Come here, Pyrros. Pay no attention to these children."

The fire in the cat's eyes faded as it withdrew to Cleopatra to have its head stroked. Its colouring faded. Once again it looked more like a large cat than a monster.

"This cat is wild but he obeys me - only me," said Cleopatra. "He is unique and ancient. The bond with my family was forged in battle and is renewed with blood in every generation of my family. I will not be crossed, nor will my cat."

For a moment both Harry and Eleanor saw her eyes burn with the same fire that they had seen in the cat's eyes. But in a human, the pin-shaped centre turned Cleopatra into a monster.

71

Harry had seen eyes like that only this morning. At a distance, they were inhuman. At this close range, they seemed to pierce his soul. They terrified him.

"Do you understand?"

Both children nodded, too frightened to speak.

"Now tell me. How did you get into the chamber and what were you doing there?"

Neither of the children were going to tell the Queen exactly how they arrived, not only because they were frightened but also because they thought they would seem ridiculous. An out-of-control lift and time travel were absurd.

Harry spoke first. He wasn't a good liar, so he stuck to as much of the truth as he could: "We just followed you in." Just in time he added, "Your Majesty."

"Rubbish," she spat. "You, girl. Where are you from?"

"England," Eleanor answered.

"Ing-land? I have never heard of it. Blue eyes in Egypt belong to strangers. You are foreign magicians. You came to steal the secrets of the Scroll. And how can you read it? No one now living knows the language of the Scroll. Who is your master? You will tell me - I will have you tortured until you tell the truth. Guards!"

The door opened and the guards stood to attention in the doorway. Cleopatra said, "These blue-eyed magicians shall go to the private dungeon in the Palace. We will learn more from them there. March them across to the Palace now with Caesar and myself. Do not trust them. Do not let anyone else speak to them, or I will have your skins."

The Queen turned and swept out with her cat.

13. Fire!

Surrounded by guards, Harry and Eleanor marched across the ramparts overlooking the harbour in the wake of Caesar and Cleopatra. Behind them Harry could see the priest and the soothsayer, walking just behind Caesar, who was speaking to them. He was trying to hear what they were saying, when a blast of hot air knocked the children off their feet into the guards at their sides, and there was a massive explosion. The whole party stopped abruptly and the guards closed up around them. Below the ramparts, the damage was clear.

One of the larger galleys was split into two pieces. Fire snaked up the rigging, leaping from rope to rope. Bone-dry sails caught fire, burning rags floating like falling stars before dropping into the sea. The flames did not die out as the wreckage hit the water. Instead, they spread out like a carpet of oil across the sea and burnt even more fiercely.

An unnatural silence followed the huge explosion, before another smaller conflagration burst from the bows of the wreck, spreading more havoc. Small pockets of flame arced over the harbour-wall and landed on the sea beyond. Instead of extinguishing it, the water seemed to feed the fire.

Chaos broke out. Soldiers and staff came running to Caesar and Cleopatra for orders. In the harbour every effort to douse the flames was futile, and at least one other galley had caught fire. It was sinking below the water, leaving another carpet of flames above it. Other galley commanders had more sense and the galley-slaves were being whipped into action to take the ships out to sea, away from the danger.

"Why doesn't it go out?" asked Eleanor.

The thin priest in front of her heard her remark. He said, "It is magic fire, a secret the Greeks knew of, but never fully developed. Water has no effect on it."

"Silence!" snapped the guard. "No talking to the prisoners."

Caesar was shouting at a subordinate, "What idiot was experimenting in the harbour? I was promised the weapon would be developed properly! That engineer will not live to see another night!"

At that moment, Neos ran up the rampart staircase. He darted past the soldiers to the spot where Cleopatra and Caesar were standing. "Mother! Caesar, sir!" he started.

Caesar looked fit to explode at the interruption. "What makes you think you can interrupt me, boy?"

"But sir! I met a strange girl - "

"Not now!" interrupted Cleopatra.

"No, not now!" roared Caesar. "Have you no concept of time or place?"

The boy looked up defiantly at the general who had won the heart of his mother. If he didn't want to know about the strange girl he had met, that was fine. He wouldn't know about the girl. Neos stood still, like a soldier at attention and waited. He would bide his time. He noticed the other two children and saw their blue eyes. He knew there must be some connection, but still he stayed silent, fuming.

Caesar snapped his fingers to bring the priest and the

soothsayer to his side. "These two children must be questioned carefully," he said.

"I have already given orders," began Cleopatra, but Caesar was not listening. He went on, "They are in your custody. Tell no one but the Queen and me what they say." He looked specifically at the soothsayer. "Do whatever - whatever - you must to find out what they know!" Harry flinched when he saw the eager look on the soothsayer's face. "Split them up to start with. Interrogate them separately. Soothsayer, take the boy. You, priest, take the girl." Caesar had finished giving his orders and turned to Cleopatra, "We must go."

Neos looked at the other two children intently. They stared back at him. Then the soothsayer, said simply, "Come."

"I'm not leaving Eleanor," Harry said, grabbing her hand.

"You are," said the soothsayer. He took a sharp hold on Harry's earlobe and dragged him.

"Stop that! It hurts!" Harry clamped his hand to his ear over the soothsayer's hand, feeling a wet patch of blood trickle down the side of his head. Eleanor let out a cry. The soothsayer pinched his earlobe more tightly.

"Next time," he sneered, bending down towards Harry and giving the ear another tug, "I'll pull your ear off. And that will just be the beginning. Now are you coming quietly or not?"

Harry knew this wasn't the moment to fight. "Yeah, all right!" The soothsayer let go of his ear and Harry's hand shot up to rub the pain away, feeling the sticky blood on his fingers. He turned to give what he hoped might be a reassuring glance to Eleanor, but got a whack on the back of his head: "Now!"

"Harry!" called Eleanor despairingly as he was taken down some stairs - to a dungeon, she assumed. She saw Neos follow them, and wondered why.

The gaunt priest had moved to stand beside her. His thick hair was unmarked by grey, but his eyes were shrunk deep in his lined face. He was taller than most of the Egyptians she had seen around the Palace. He lifted his hand and Eleanor flinched, certain that he was going to hit her. She moved backwards to avoid the blow, but to her surprise he laid his elegant, long-fingered hand upon her shoulder.

"Look up at me," he said gently. She did so, and saw that his eyes were full of depth and wisdom. "You need to trust me. I am not going to hurt you."

Every instinct of Eleanor's told her not to trust this man. So did everything she had been taught about strangers who might try to trap her with kindness. She turned and ran. She ran straight into a legionary. It might just as well have been a stone wall. The legionary did not move, merely absorbed the impact, seized her by the scruff of the neck and handed her back to the priest.

The priest did not laugh, or say anything, but instead said simply, "We will go into the Great Library. It will be more comfortable there than the dungeon." He turned to the guards, "I will not need you to accompany me." Then he beckoned Eleanor and said, "Follow me."

14. Sacred Crocodiles

As the priest led Eleanor down the stairs, she rubbed her head where it had bumped on the legionary's armour. Should she make another run for it? But where could she go? All the doors were guarded by burly centurions.

"Keep with me and they will not interfere with us," said the priest as if he was reading her mind. Eleanor noticed that he said "us," not you. Why would he say that to a prisoner?

They approached the main door of the Library. Long stone steps led up towards huge columns fronting a massive double door at the front of the building. It reminded Eleanor of a visit she had once made to St Paul's Cathedral in London, except there was no majestic dome.

As the priest and Eleanor approached the door, two guards stood to attention, and the door suddenly opened inwards like an automatic gate. It had been opened from the inside. Someone must have been waiting there watching for them to arrive.

"I thought you might like the ceremonial entrance," said the priest. "It's only used for special guests." He didn't sound sarcastic, but Eleanor hoped that 'special' didn't mean 'about to be tortured'. But why the main gates then? She didn't feel that she was a special guest at all. After all, she was a prisoner. Closing doors ought to make you feel like you were in a prison, but here the closing of the doors changed the atmosphere. The chaos and madness of the siege and the fire outside were gone. They were standing in a large colonnaded antechamber, open to the sky. In the centre was a rectangular pool of water with a sort of well-head in the middle. For some reason lighted lamps had been placed around the pool.

"It's peaceful here," Eleanor said.

"The soldiers are not allowed in here," replied the priest as if the two things were related.

Drawn to the calm of the water, Eleanor went towards the pool and looked down. She thought she saw steam rising off the water.

The priest said, "The water is kept heated. It keeps them happy."

Eleanor knelt down with her hand outstretched to the pool. There was not a ripple on it. The priest grasped her shoulder and pulled her back.

"That is not wise. I too am always drawn to the pool, but you must not touch the water."

"Why not?"

"We will wait a moment and you will see. They are always fed just after sunset. Stand back from the pool now. This always makes me feel uncomfortable, even though I should have become used to it by now."

At that moment, doors at the other end of the room were opened. Eleanor thought she could see a bubble or two in the water, like a fish rising in a river. Four men came in, carrying a great wooden tray like a stretcher and placed it near the pool. The table was piled high with bones and with raw meat. A putrid whiff struck Eleanor's nose. Some of it was clearly not quite fresh. The bones were thrown into the pool by the four men and they quickly jumped back from the side.

A moment before, the water had been like glass. Now the surface boiled as creatures from below surged up from below, fighting over the meat. Crocodiles. She shuddered with the thought of how close she had come to putting her hand into the water.

"These," said the priest, "are the sacred crocodiles of the Ptolemaic pharaohs of Egypt. They have lived here in the entrance to the library for generations and it is the task of the librarians to feed them every day. A most unusual task for a librarian, I am sure you will agree. Thankfully, I was relieved of this duty some time ago."

"Are you a librarian, then?" asked Eleanor tentatively, still with her eyes on the pool. She realised that she had not felt like a prisoner since they entered the building, yet he was supposed to be her guard.

"Yes," he said. "Come, we will go to my study. Then we have some secrets to share."

As they left the pool, the surface was becoming still again as the crocodiles sank under the water and returned to their lairs to eat.

"This is the copying room," said the priest, rather like a tour guide, as they entered the next chamber. Row upon row of flat cushions were spread across a marble floor with tiny desks in front of them. Only one or two were occupied by men writing with long reeds. "If we were not at war, there would be hundreds of scribes at work here, even at night, with inadequate lamp-light to see by, copying out scrolls for the library. Our laws say that every ship that stops in our port cannot leave until it is searched for books. The books are seized and copied for the library, but it has to be done quickly otherwise it would also affect Alexandria's position at the centre of the world's trade. In five hundred years of this practice, the library has become the greatest in the world. Our scribes can work in over forty languages, and most of them can speak five or six. But the poor light is a burden on their eyesight. One day I hope there will be a better way." He sighed. "The war between Cleopatra and her brother has put a stop to that. It is a tragedy for the library, but not as great as the tragedy to come. That is why I am so glad to have found you."

"What do you mean?" asked Eleanor, surprised by what this man was saying.

He put a finger to his lips. "Not here. We must go to my study."

The study was a small room with one window high up. Even with the lamps lit, it was dark. The walls were lined with racks containing what appeared to be wooden circles. Eleanor was reminded, with a pang of nostalgia, of Great Uncle Jasper's wine cellar. The three children had found their way there one day playing hide and seek - and hiding from Horrible Hair Bun. But the wooden circles were not the ends of bottles. As Eleanor looked around, she realised that these were the ends of scrolls, stacked horizontally in the racks. Books as she knew them didn't exist here. They were all scrolls, long sheets of papyrus rolled up for storage. She thought they must be cumbersome to read.

The priest dropped to a cushion on the floor and sat cross-legged. He signalled to Eleanor to do the same.

"You must forgive me," he said. "I haven't spoken to any children for such a long time, so I'm not sure how. I'll just have to talk to you like an adult. What's more, I imagine you think you're my prisoner."

"Aren't I a prisoner?"

"Well yes, you are. But you're not my prisoner. You're Caesar and Cleopatra's prisoner. You should trust me. I know that's going to be hard to do, so when I said we're going to share some secrets, I realise I'm going to have to start."

Eleanor wondered where all this was going. "OK."

The priest looked a little nervous. "I've never told anyone this before. No one knows. Well, no one living anyway."

There was a pause. Eleanor didn't know what to say, but also felt she ought to speak, so she said, "OK" again.

"OK?" said the priest. "What does 'OK' mean?"

"OK?" replied Eleanor. "Well it means, OK. That's silly, isn't it?" She paused. "It means 'That's fine,' I suppose."

"OK, then," said the priest with a smile. "My name is Nicomachus. I'm nearly four hundred years old."

Eleanor looked at the dark hair without a hint of grey and then at his eyes, deep in their sockets, which shone with the wisdom of experience. She wondered if he dyed his hair.

"Er - OK."

"You don't appear surprised. Most people would be. Are you surprised?"

"No," replied Eleanor.

"Do you know many people as old as me?"

If this really was an interrogation, Eleanor thought, this might be the moment to lie or to invent a story, but he was such a strange man, she thought she would tell the truth. What harm could it do now?

"Just one, but he's a lot older than you. He's a librarian too."

15. Nicomachus

Eleanor didn't know what to think of this gentle old man. He appeared to be trusted by Cleopatra and Caesar. Since they were her enemies, this man should be her enemy too, but he didn't seem to be. She wanted to know more about him, but there was a much more pressing question, one which needed to be asked quickly before she thought about it too much.

"What are they going to do to Harry?"

Nicomachus did not reply. He stood up and reached for a shelf and pulled down a blanket. "Are you cold? I am. I think it's my age." Eleanor thought back to the ridiculous way Harry had arrived for breakfast that morning, dressed in a heavy coat, cap and scarf to protect him from the cold. It had been cold in England for sure, but here in Alexandria it was boiling.

Eleanor looked at the priest as he wrapped himself in a blanket. He had taken something else down from the shelf as well. Circular and silvery, it looked like a mirror. Why was he staring at himself? This was hardly the time for vanity.

She waited a moment but couldn't contain herself. "What about Harry? Are they going to torture him?"

The priest looked silently into the circular object. It infuriated Eleanor. "Why don't you say something?"

Nicomachus put the thing gently on the floor beside him

again. "Harry will be safe, though I cannot see well enough to know if he is comfortable just now. You will both be safe - for now at least, but the journey will be hard. I'm not so sure about me, but that's always so much harder to see. I think it's like talking about yourself. It can be quite embarrassing, for some people at least. Caesar of course writes about himself in the third person all the time. It's an ego thing." He paused, looking into the mirror again, puzzled. "There are three of you?" He looked up at her. "You have another friend here?"

Eleanor blurted out excitedly: "Is Grace here? Really? How do you know?"

"I have a gift of foresight. They call it a gift anyway. I'm not convinced. I think it's more of a burden, but that's another secret I've given away. I'm not very good at this, am I? Two secrets shared with you and yet still I know nothing about you."

"What do you mean foresight? And how do you know about Grace?"

"The mirror helps me see briefly into the near future, but it's never clear. It also helps me to see the past about some people, which does tend to be much clearer, but then hindsight is always easier for everyone, isn't it? Sometimes I'm wrong about my predictions, but that's usually because strong-willed people can change their own destiny - and those of others. I can only see things that are happening a short way ahead. It's like being in a fog. You can only see so far with occasional glimpses when the mist clears for a moment."

"And Grace?" asked Eleanor, too interested in her cousin to be diverted even by something as exciting as a magic mirror.

"I can see all together here in Alexandria. The strange thing is, I don't have any feeling for your past. Most unusual. Normally, I have a glimpse into people's past as well as their future and then

I can put things together, but not you."

"But where's Grace?"

He smiled gently. "She's close, I feel. But it's time for you to tell me something about you, isn't it?"

Fine, thought Eleanor, if that's how he wants to play it, I'll tell him the truth, though I bet he won't believe it.

She said, "I'm from the future and so is Harry."

Instead of being dismissive as she expected, he looked at her with an almost youthful grin. "Tell me then - how did you get here?"

"We fell down a lift-shaft from The Palace Library after letting the White Phoenix in through the window."

"The same White Phoenix that was seen in Alexandria today?"

"Yes."

Nicomachus let out a long breath. "So there is hope. Hope at a time of desperation when I believed all was lost. There is a magic in the libraries that connects us. I am now too old and compromised to carry on with my burden now. Just when I thought all was lost!"

"I'm not sure I like the sound of that."

"We do not all chose our fate, but we can make the most of our journey. That is the challenge of life. You must grasp it!" He was excited now.

Eleanor thought she liked that advice even less. "So you believe me?"

"Of course, it's the only explanation that fits. We have seen two Phoenixes today. That cruel soothsayer of Caesar's barely recognised the bird."

Eleanor looked blankly at him. "I don't understand."

"There is only ever one Phoenix at a time. The first was born at Creation, but every thousand years or so the bird is reborn in fire. This is a bird with no mate, a lonely bird, but the most magical, intelligent and wise bird in existence. If there were two Phoenixes, as there were today, the second can only have come from the future or the past. The Phoenix in our time is golden. Something strange has happened in your time to make the Phoenix white." The priest was alive with excitement. "You must be the hope I have been looking for at a time of great gloom. Thank you. But we must be very careful."

Eleanor's mind was a turmoil. She had a thousand questions to ask, but was shaken even more by his next remark. He leant down and grasped her hand firmly as if to emphasise the point. "You must be warned about your own time though. A Phoenix is only reborn with white plumage at a time of great turmoil. You must prepare yourself when you get home."

"How can we get home then?"

"I don't know. I cannot see that. But I have a great deal to tell you now I know who you are."

Great, thought Eleanor to herself. Now I have to listen to him even more when we need to be rescuing Harry!

16. The Battle with the Cat

Nicomachus pointed to his left eye. Eleanor had been watching it. It never moved. "I lost this in the battle with the cat in the foothills of the mountains, far, far East. Have you met the cat? You'll have seen it at Cleopatra's side. Strange colouring, so that sometimes it appears invisible."

Eleanor looked down at her arm and ran her finger up her arm where the cat had scratched her. It was puffy and hot to touch.

"Yes. I've met the cat," replied Eleanor. "I wish I hadn't."

"Sometimes I wish that too, but our fate and destiny is not always in our own hands."

You can say that again, she thought, homesick for England and her real life. "Do you believe in fate?" she asked.

"That's the sort of question Aristotle used to ask us at school," sighed the old man, ignoring the question. "He was the sort of teacher you never appreciated until it was too late."

"So? Do you?" said Eleanor, having a vague feeling she'd heard of the name Aristotle, but certainly having no idea where.

"Of course, but fate only guides us. We can change things at any time. That's why I think it's impossible really to see into the future. This magic mirror gives me an idea of what might happen, but people can control their own destinies and take charge of their lives. Most people don't really do that though. Alexander was different - one of the most dynamic leaders ever and he took charge of the fate of thousands of people. That's why we call him 'The Great.' Let me tell you about the battle with the cat. Pyrros is its name, but its story is much older and bound up with mine and our fate today."

"Yes?"

"Perhaps that was the moment my fate changed - over four hundred years ago. I had been a champion at school. That was why I was sent to King Philip's court. I won a challenge in our village. I was the strongest, the best fighter." Nicomachus held up his hands with a pride that defied his fragile frame. "These knuckles are not bent and worn by age! They are the fists of a champion! As a twelve-year-old boy, I had muscles that would enable me to defeat boys six or seven years older than me. You may not believe it now, but I could. Then I was sent to the Palace and since I was the same age as Alexander I went to school with him. Alexander and I became close friends as far as our different upbringing allowed. We learnt about science and the arts. We learnt astronomy and astrology. Our teacher was Aristotle. That's fate," said Nicomachus. "I was a village boy, a fighter and I ended up in the same school as the greatest general the world has ever seen, taught by one of the most famous teachers out of Athens. I was there with Ptolemy, who would later be Alexander's right-hand man and is Cleopatra's ancestor. But those people changed the world and now alone I protect Alexander's legacy." Then he shrank into himself and looked disappointed. "Even my foresight cannot help now."

"Tell me about the cat," said Eleanor, and then blushed as her tummy rumbled loudly. It seemed a long time since the marshmallows in The Palace Library.

Nicomachus said, "You are hungry! I'm sorry, I didn't think - you must eat." He rummaged in his desk and produced some dates and a piece of dry-looking cheese, which he sliced with a knife from his desk. He put the food on a piece of papyrus and pushed it across to Eleanor. She took a piece of cheese and said, "What about you?"

"Thank you, I have eaten," he said politely.

The cheese was salty, but good. With her mouth full, Eleanor said, "Do go on with the story."

"The cat was really when my fate changed. Until then I had been part of Alexander's bodyguard. We protected him and his close generals - the men like Ptolemy - in the battles. We had never been defeated. He never was, but he was becoming increasingly obsessed with tales we heard on our campaigns about creatures of the underworld - The Nether World - as he kept referring to it. These were not like the fiercest of animals that roam the wildest parts of earth. These were creatures that had been born shortly after the beginning of time, but they were not born from the creation of the world by the gods. They were the heinous offspring of their mistakes. The tribes that were exiled from Egypt generations ago refer to them as the Sons of Cain, the monsters that sprang from the union of the man who murdered his brother shortly after creation. These are the creatures of The Nether World.

"The further east we went, the more often we heard the stories. We met the wise men, the holy men and the outcasts from the villages in the places we conquered. These were the men who, it was rumoured, could defeat the great Alexander after their armies had been beaten. They would summon the creatures and control them, said the villagers.

"Anyway, everyone thought this was nonsense. Except

Alexander. He was obsessed by it all along and believed it. He was desperate to remain unconquered forever and wanted to consider every way, magical, mythical or just nonsense. It was insane.

"Then we met the cat.

"It was in a mountainous region as far east as we ever marched. The warriors were strong but we defeated them. But the villagers' stories were more frequent and the priests' stories were more convincing. There they painted third eyes on their foreheads - the better to see into The Nether World.

"At first, the cat marauded at night. Soldier after soldier vanished and then the cat became braver and started attacking the camp in the day. Some of our strongest guards were taken and we could make no progress. While we delayed, the troops of our enemy grew stronger and stronger and threatened to drive us away - the very thing that Alexander feared most. So the entire army became focused on defeating the cat. Can you imagine that? The greatest army in the world delayed by attacking a cat?

"We were in the mountains when it happened. Ptolemy was commanding a small group looking for the animal to the flank of Alexander's main guard. The animal leapt from above us. It jumped out of a group of rocks high up. A small avalanche of rocks were all the warning we had of its coming. Then it was in front of me. The hair on its back was raised and it growled. I remember seeing its eyes in front of me. A slither of black with actual fire burning within it. Then it leapt at me. I was not its target. It sensed Ptolemy as the commander, but whilst it leapt right over me and out of my reach, its claws shot out of its paws and struck me in the left eye. That was the last time I saw out of this eye. I saw the fight with Ptolemy out of the other eye. That was when my fate changed. When all of our fates changed."

"Ptolemy and the cat stood face to face. Those brown and red stripes blended into the colours of the desert rocks. Ptolemy's sword was drawn. Then he hissed to the guard around him: 'Withdraw. This is my fight.' It was to be a single combat with the wild beast. Ptolemy threw down his long sword and drew a simple short dagger from his waist - the same dagger Cleopatra wears today. The cat had no weapons at all, but its claws were filled with a powerful venom. And its teeth, uncovered only when it opens its powerful jaw, are terrifying." Eleanor shuddered, thinking of her own brief encounter in the cells, but Nicomachus just kept telling his story without noticing.

"Ptolemy made the first move, leaping from a pile of stones where he found the advantage of height. He came down on the cat's head smothering it with his body before the cat was able to open its jaws. The dagger struck behind the neck, but the cat whipped its legs out from behind and struck Ptolemy's face scratching him deep from his forehead to his jaw.

"Then both the cat and Ptolemy stood circling again, blood dripping from both of them to the rocks. The guard closed in but once again Ptolemy said, 'He is mine.' This time it was the cat's turn to pounce, but Ptolemy crouched underneath and the dagger plunged deep into its heart. Ptolemy pulled himself out from under the body of the beast, but then he was on his knees, weak from the fight and suffering from the venomous scratch, which was swelling up in great purple blisters. On his knees he crawled to the beast and withdrew his dagger before standing up and looking down at his conquest.

"The guard relaxed and his lieutenant came and slapped him on the back in congratulations. But the creature came back to life. It just licked its wounds and they stopped bleeding. The lieutenant had drawn his sword to kill it, but Ptolemy stopped him. Then the cat came to towards Ptolemy. It was extraordinary. It stretched itself out in front of him in submission. Then the cat lifted itself on its rear feet and gently placed them on Ptolemy's shoulders. It licked the wound on his face and as it did so, those giant blisters subsided and all that left was a faint scar.

"That was when the cat became Ptolemy's servant and the servant of Ptolemy's descendants. But although Ptolemy had conquered beast, in the end the beast also conquered Ptolemy with its evil influence. The venom must have entered his soul for after that his character changed. He became egotistical, power hungry and without mercy.

"The cat was never apart from his conqueror, but Ptolemy's eyes changed too. When he was angry - and he became angry a lot - his eyes became like the cat's, filled with an orange fire."

"I saw that in Cleopatra's eyes too!" exclaimed Eleanor.

"Yes, the bond is renewed with each generation with the venom of the cat. The darkness has entered Neos's soul. The cat is a monstrous beast that never dies, but its evil influence from the beginnings of creation lives on within it and the ancestors of Ptolemy."

"But what happened to you? Why did it change your fate and your life?"

"The battle with the cat had two consequences. It confirmed the existence of such creatures. These were no longer creatures of myth but of reality. Alexander's personal obsession became a mission. And I became the one to gather the information on our travels. I could no longer fight so well with one eye. I had the trust of Alexander and the education Aristotle had given us, so I was the one to gather as information and the wisdom - evil or not - from as many sources as possible. Not only did we create an empire, but we gathered the scrolls and materials that lie at the heart of this library at Alexandria - the greatest library the world has ever known."

"There was one Scroll that was more important than any other. It was the Scroll you saw earlier today, so important that Alexander later entrusted me on his deathbed to protect it with my life. We didn't initially know its importance when we found the temple high in the mountains that housed it. To this day I have lived with the guilt that it was taken by force and its guardians died trying to stop us removing it. The last breath of those guardians was not of hatred or condemnation though. The dying breath was of pleading. They pleaded with Alexander to protect the information in the Scroll. It was too dangerous to fall in the wrong hands, but it was also too important to destroy. The king and I were alone when we found the Scroll and even then Ptolemy was noticeably changing for the worse, so we agreed to keep it secret. Ptolemy and the rest of the soldiers were too busy plundering the gold and treasures of the temple to be bothered with an old Scroll.

"It wasn't until later that we realised the significance of the Scroll, for it was written in a language we found impossible to read. Only later did we discover how to read it. Only then did we understand. Only then did we realise the power of this book. And Alexander entrusted its protection to me, a job I have done for nearly 400 years. Now I am failing and the forces of evil and Ptolemy's ancestors are winning."

Eleanor was gripped now. "How can a single book be so important? How could one simple document be so dangerous?"

"The Scroll contained all the information Alexander and I had been looking for. Until that point we only had scraps - bits and pieces. This Scroll had centuries - millennia even - of knowledge that the temple priests had collected and sworn to protect. It contains secrets about the creatures of The Nether World. It contains the secrets of how to draw the evil creatures from their lairs, into our world. And it contains the secrets of how to both control and destroy those creatures. In the wrong hands, it allows evil to dominate the world."

"But why didn't you just destroy it?"

"We talked about it, and laboured over whether that was the best thing. Alexander was a visionary emperor and a great general. Sometimes there were misdeeds and he was certainly far from perfect, but he would never have been drawn to using evil magic for his own use. The problem was that there were others who would - and Ptolemy was certainly becoming one. We both knew that some of the information in the book could be obtained elsewhere, even from the other scrolls we collected. If kings and emperors with evil in their hearts did manage to draw the monsters from the depths of The Nether World, other would need the knowledge in our book to fight them and destroy the creatures. It contains the key to fighting evil. That is why we could not destroy it. But now? Now I wonder if I might have to."

Eleanor sat still, thinking. She looked at old Nicomachus and thought about what he was saying and what she had heard. She thought about the previous summer and she began to consider something and wonder if she now knew why they were really here. But she needed to test something. If Nicomachus had the means to read the Scroll, he must have done exactly that. He would know the secrets within it. "So, this book. This book would tell you how to subdue a dragon. It would tell you, say, that you need a sword forged in a volcano to kill it." She said this casually, as if she was just making it up, like writing a short story at school. Eleanor wanted to see Nicomachus's reaction.

He smiled. It was a smile of relief as if a burden had been lifted. "Yes, yes. But you know this, don't you? You're not making it up as you pretend?"

Eleanor nodded.

"I am right then. You are here for the Scroll. Perhaps the magic of the Scroll has brought you here itself."

17. Harry and Neos

Harry decided the soothsayer just enjoyed inflicting pain, as he pulled his ear. It certainly was an effective way of keeping him under control.

Either way, Harry ended up in a dungeon in a far worse and far more uncomfortable state than Eleanor. An urgent message came for the soothsayer to attend on Caesar, a summons that could not be ignored. Then Harry was left alone, locked in the cell. The sleeve of his gown was now covered in drying blood from his ear.

The soothsayer's steps were still echoing at the further end of the corridor, when Harry heard a noise at the door. Bolts were drawn back. Neos stood there with a smile, "Shall we go and look at the fire then?"

Harry desperately wanted to escape, but he was so surprised that he questioned it, "How can we? And what about the guard?"

Neos laughed. "They wouldn't dare stop me!" He reached into a pocket and pulled out a small silver coin. Holding it in front of Harry's face, he added, "They're terribly badly paid anyway. It'll be worth his while."

Neos banged on the door and called the guard. "We're going up to the ramparts," said Neos, thrusting the coin into his hand. There was a moment's hesitation but it was all so simple. Harry was amazed as the guard stepped aside. What he didn't see in the dull light of the cell was the way the colour dropped out of the soldier's face. He didn't see the orange fire in the eyes of Neos. The soldier was not bribed by money but by fear of the supernatural.

Harry felt a surge of relief leaving the cell. Perhaps there was some hope of freedom after all. He knew the boy was the son of Cleopatra but Harry had noticed the way he had been put down by Caesar. Maybe there was a chance he would be an ally.

"I'm Harry," he shouted as they ran up the stairs.

"Neos," said the other, turning his head with a cheerful grin.

"We need to find Eleanor," said Harry.

"Later!" replied Neos dashing ahead.

Neos led the way out of the dungeons and darted this way and that through a maze of corridors that led them out of the library complex. He occasionally turned to check that Harry had kept up with him, but he didn't say another word. When they were clear of the main buildings, he paused and they both caught their breath. "I don't know if you've ever noticed," said Neos, "but adults often completely ignore us when we're not causing trouble, especially when they're busy. We need to cross the courtyard and then get out of the gate. Let's walk around the edge of the square. Look as if you belong here."

Harry wasn't going to argue. He was free. As they reached the main gate, Neos stopped again. There were legionaries all around and the guard at the gate noticed everyone coming in and out of the complex. Neos whispered. "I really want to avoid being seen at all, but it's unavoidable here, so now we'll have to stand tall and leave together. I don't think they would dare challenge me."

So they went, side by side, and Harry pretended to look

as if he should be there. As they passed through the gate, the legionaries either side of the main passage suddenly drew their feet together and raised their tall spears. Harry's heart beat fast, but he stared straight ahead and did as Neos said. Neos looked to the left and right and waved at them - and then he looked at Harry and hissed, "They're just saluting us. Come on!"

Near the edge of the harbour, a great causeway stood before them, joining the land to an island in the sea. To the west was the port where the ship had exploded. There was no sign of the fire any more, but outside the harbour a few of the galleys that had fled to safety were beginning to return. Ahead, at the other end of the causeway, a huge building towered above them, high as the spire of Salisbury Cathedral. A vast flame was lit at its peak now that it was dusk. Harry stared in awe. It was the lighthouse of Pharos, one of the wonders of the world.

"Come on. We're going to the lighthouse on the island. I've only been up there once but you can see for miles - and it can be seen for miles." Neos added, "I've been to the island lots though. We won't take the road. We need to climb up to the side of the aqueduct and then run along the wall. We'll never get caught. No one ever looks up!"

Huge boulders were not much of an obstacle to the agile boys and they soon reached a wall at the top. Harry's heart started to beat faster. He didn't like heights. To the right lay a huge drop into the sea, the farther side from the harbour, shaded in darkness with some scary looking rocks. To the left, some eight metres below them, was an aqueduct. The wall was just fifteen centimetres thick. And as Harry quickly discovered, many of the stones at the top were loose and crumbling. It was about a two hundred metre run to the other side, and a strong breeze blowing from the land didn't help. One stone slipped off the top off the wall when they were halfway across. Harry looked down as it landed in the aqueduct. Looking down at all was, he discovered, a mistake and he shut his eyes before looking up. Neos was far ahead.

Then something else caught Harry's eye. Coming in from the sea, lit by flames from the lighthouse and by the moon which was rising ahead of them, there was a huge turbulence in the sea, a silent wave gathering pace. Something was swimming at speed under the water. The waves twisted towards one of the galleys, which suddenly swayed and turned on the spot as if spun by a giant. A huge serpent reared its head out of the water. It wound its tail around the bow of the boat and shook it. On board, Harry saw some sailors lining up in defence. Then the sea-serpent snatched one of the men off the deck. Its jaws took the body and tossed it in the air before catching it again. Then the serpent vanished below the water with its prey. A strange calm ensued with ripples circling from the boat as if a stone had been thrown into a pond and vanished.

Harry looked towards Neos again and saw he had reached the other side. Being on top of the wall was obviously one of the worst places to be just now. Harry looked straight ahead and ran, ignoring everything else, even the stones slipping beneath his feet.

Breathless, Harry met Neos was on the far end of the aqueduct the other side.

"Where have you been?" Neos asked abruptly. "Did you see?"

"What is it?" asked Harry.

"I don't know but there have been rumours about what my uncle Ptolemy has been doing. They say he can summon creatures from the darkest parts of the world to do battle for him against my mother. Perhaps this is one of them."

Harry looked blankly at Neos. "Your uncle? Why is he attacking your mother?"

Neos looked strangely back at Harry. "Where are you from? Don't you know anything?" He didn't wait for an answer. "My uncle is at war with my mother over who should rule Egypt. My uncle doesn't think the Romans should be here and is determined to stop them. He hates Caesar. Come to think of it, so do I, but Cleopatra is my mother and is the true Queen. Caesar is saving her throne. Look now!"

The sea churned again and the serpent lifted its head out of the water, hungry for another victim. This time, the sailors were more prepared. Either side of the galley, they were manned with swords, spears and axes and protected with shields. The serpent had a sinewy neck and head and Harry could see its power was in its enormous jaws, lined with sharp teeth. This time it could not grab a man so easily as it darted towards the boat.

Several archers shot arrows into its neck. They had no effect except to make it more angry, then Harry saw that the arrows were attached to ropes and other sailors were hauling the serpent's head towards them, hooked like a fish. A brave axeman stood on the side of the galley and hacked away at the serpent's neck until its head fell away and dropped into the sea.

Neos cheered. "That'll show it, and that'll show my Uncle. Monsters can't defeat us!"

The black blood of the creature running down the side of the ship in the flickering light of the lighthouse made a gory picture. Suddenly, the serpent leapt out of the sea again. This time there were three heads; and this time the serpent made a meal of three sailors.

"Oh my God!" said Harry, forgetting everything he had ever been told about swearing. "It's a Hydra!"

"A what?" said Neos.

"A Hydra. Every time you cut its head off, it grows three more. The only way to defeat it is to burn the stumps of the heads." This time the galley was spared a shaking, but the tumultuous wake of the Hydra showed it was making straight for the harbour.

"How do you know about that?" replied Neos.

"I read about it," Harry said cautiously, remembering exactly where he had read about it last, in the Scroll on Alexander's tomb, just before he was captured.

"If you know that, we need to tell them. Come on! We need to tell them!"

"No!" said Harry, "I need to escape. Don't let them recapture me!" He was pleading. Neos stared at Harry, as if uncertain what to do next. He hesitated long enough for Harry to understand that Neos might not be such a friend after all. He wondered what calculation Neos was making in his mind. He said, "Please."

Suddenly Neos smiled. "Of course," he said. "You hide here and I'll come back to get you later."

Another voice replied from behind them. The bitter, sarcastic voice of the soothsayer. "I think not. You'll both come with me."

There was only one thing the boys could do. They ran the other way.

18. Ordeal by Hydra

It was useless to run. Two legionaries grabbed the boys. Neos was immediately released when they realised who he was, but the soothsayer once more used Harry's ear to drag him along.

With his ear in that harsh grip, Harry hung his head to one side to make it less painful and fixed his mind on the lighthouse. It was an amazing building, a huge square block with an octagonal tower above it. On top of that was a much simpler circular tower housing the flame that guided ships into the great port of Alexandria, the greatest port in the world. Except now it was the most dangerous port in the world.

Even if Caesar had not been wearing his purple toga, Harry would have identified him as the leader. He stood tall amongst his senior staff, who were gathered at the edge of the lighthouse island on a platform above the water. The water stilled for a moment, a lull while the serpent digested its victims.

Neos ran up to Caesar with haughty defiance. Caesar's staff dared not touch him. Before he was even spoken to, he volunteered the information, "This boy Harry knows what this serpent is."

"Sir," roared Caesar.

"Sir," replied Neos, defiantly, but it could barely be heard over the sound of Caesar's continued roar.

"This boy should be in the dungeon, not with you. Whichever

soldier let your wily ways persuade him to let you out will suffer! I assume you did release him."

"I did … sir, but that's not important."

"I will be the judge of that," said Caesar. "Well? Speak then, and tell me!"

"The thing in the harbour - it is a Hydra … sir."

"Pah," said Caesar scornfully.

"He knows how to kill it too." Neos explained what Harry had said.

"And I suppose you think this information is why I should treat you leniently for this continued disobedience?"

Neos looked hopeful for a moment. "Yes, sir."

"Well think again. You are a fool. You always have been and you always will be. If you had paid attention or bothered to turn up to listen to your Greek tutor, you would know the same thing. You would not be surprised at what this other boy says. Tell him, soothsayer."

The soothsayer said as scornfully as Caesar, "This is one of the creatures that Hercules slew. We all know how to deal with it. We do not need the interference of a child like you."

"Exactly," said Caesar. "Take them away. No. Wait. Bring that stranger here. We will test the foreign magician."

Caesar bent down to Harry and spoke so that no one else could hear, "I would not send Neos into danger. He is the apple of Cleopatra's eye. You, on the other hand, were reading from the secret Scroll and I do not know where you are from. What are you? Are you a spy for my enemies or are you sent by the gods to confound me?"

Harry hardly knew what to say. Caesar interpreted his silence as defiance.

"No answer, eh? Well, I have no more time for questioning.

We will test you now. If you are a spy or a magician, you will survive this next ordeal by your wits or your knowledge. You then may be of some use before I execute you. If you are no good, you will surely die and I will not need to waste my time with you and that girl." He snapped his fingers and his guards sprang to attention. "This boy will go in the boat with the others to face the Hydra. Prepare it now." Caesar turned away.

Harry shivered. He had always admired Caesar when he'd learned about him at school, but what sort of man was he to send a boy to his death? He remembered learning about Trials by Ordeal. They were always a no-win situation. If the person being tested succeeded in passing the test, they were assumed guilty and killed. If they failed, the test itself would result in death. This was going to be his fate, out in the harbour facing the monster.

"Help me Neos! Help!" yelled Harry as a last resort. Surely the boy would do something. He had helped him escape already. But Harry saw Neos just shrug his shoulders. There was no escape. Even so, Harry struggled with the soldiers who now held him, but they were so much stronger, it was hopeless.

A boat was moored at the harbour-side. In many ways it was no different to any large rowing boat manned by sailors for centuries, but Harry saw an odd machine strapped to the centre.

"Ahoy! One more to come on board," shouted one of the soldiers to the men in the boat. There was a metal ladder fixed to the side of the wall. "Down you go," said the soldier.

"No!" shouted Harry, a last defiance.

"All right then, do it the hard way," said the soldier, picking him up. "Catch!" he shouted. He threw Harry off the wall so that he crumpled in a heap in the boat.

"Steady there," said a sailor. His voice was far too cheerful for the circumstances. "What brings you aboard to join our merry crew of volunteers?"

"We're not all volunteers," grumbled a voice at the front.

"Ignore him," said the cheerful sailor. "He's our Greek Fire expert. Used to working in the dockyard, not on a boat. I'm not surprised he doesn't want to be here, since his last experiment blew up. I expect you heard that. Caesar sent him here now, saying if this boat blew up it would save him the trouble of punishing him."

Harry sat up and began to pay attention. He might as well try to save himself. "What's Greek Fire?"

"It's our secret weapon against our enemies - and maybe this monster. A special mix goes into this top cauldron, then when it gets hotter and hotter as the bellows are pumped, this nozzle throws fire out of it. Mind you, it's not just any fire. As soon as it hits the water, the flame gets bigger and bigger. The more water you add, the more it burns. Terrible it is."

Harry looked at the equipment. A metal barrel hung over a fire burning in another metal pot. The fire was blown into a furious heat by an enormous set of bellows, like a blacksmith's furnace. At the side of the barrel, a nozzle stuck out, like that on a fire hose. The nozzle had an unwieldy handle on the side and a crude mechanism to point it in all directions, around or up and down.

Harry heard the sizzling of the mix in the cauldron. Orange sparks, which might set fire to the frail wooden boat at any moment, leapt from the cauldron. One struck Harry's hand with a stabbing pinprick of pain. He was about to suck it when the sailor grabbed his hand and smothered it with a cloth. "Spit won't help with this stuff. Makes it worse. So does water. This fire eats your flesh."

"Thanks for that," muttered Harry. Then he looked up. He needed to get on with these men, to know them. "So why did you volunteer?" he said.

"Freedom. The four of us is sentenced to die next week. Fell asleep at our posts, all of us. It's a cruel world. We've been locked up in prison for a week and this is the first time we've had a chance to see the daylight, not that it's actually daylight." The man's simple optimism cheered Harry. "Caesar's spies knew Ptolemy had roused the monster. This here is a crazy plan, and we're the lucky ones to try it. What about you?"

"It's complicated," replied Harry. "What's the plan then?"

The man stopped and looked at him. "They haven't even told you?"

"Stop nattering and cast off," called another man bossily.

The cheerful sailor whispered, "I'll tell you as we go along if I can. You sit in the middle there."

Then it started.

As they rowed out to the centre of the empty harbour, the wake of the creature showed it had passed through the gates. Harry could see men at work at the entrance. "They're closing off the harbour now. It's just the beast and us."

There was a loud thwack. A huge catapult launched something over their heads. "There goes the bait - a bullock - to distract it. Hopefully eating it'll make the creature a bit sleepy before the next stage, then Mr Firemaker in the front can do his stuff when we get to work with the axes."

The dead bullock barely touched the water as the Hydra caught it with its three heads. Limbs were torn off the carcass as the Hydra's middle head bit deep into the body. Harry grabbed the gunwale as the wash from the creature slapped against the side of the boat. Bile rose in his throat and made him gag. The Hydra sank silently beneath the waters.

The cheerful sailor was unaffected. "Stage one complete.

Now they set the harbour on fire, with just poor little us in the middle. That's what all those other Greek Fire machines on the harbour walls are."

Harry tried to calm himself. Looking round for the first time, he noticed more Greek Fire machines all around the harbour's edge. One by one, they pumped out fire. As it touched the water, it spread intensely until the boat was sitting lonely in a small pool of water surrounded by fire. Harry could smell his hair being scorched and shrivelled by the heat. The same smell as burning flesh. He might have been sitting in the middle of a bonfire.

"Now let's see what that monster does!" shouted the cheerful sailor.

The monster lifted its heads through the flames to look around. Flames crackled around all its heads and its howls of pain made the hairs on Harry's neck prickle. It plunged back into the deep, killing the fire through lack of oxygen below the waves. The Hydra emerged again in a different place and now one of its heads lunged toward the little boat and the small pool of water around it. It dived down again.

"It's our turn now, boys." The sailor reached down for a huge double-headed axe. "Just keep out of my way."

The nozzle was alight, with the grumpy engineer in charge. Then suddenly the three heads with their unblinking eyes rose from the deep. The sailors picked their targets, waiting to see which head would strike first.

A sailor on the left let out a great roar, shouting "Left" as his axe swung through the air. With a sickening squelch the Hydra's head parted from its body. Then the engineer sprayed the Greek Fire from the nozzle onto the stump, cauterising the wound. But the axe-bearing sailor had to dodge the flame. The boat lurched and he lost his balance. He fell overboard, head first.

The serpent's two remaining heads darted at two targets: the sailor in the water and the engineer at the hose, snatching them as it dived below the sea.

There were just two men left in the boat with Harry now, the cheerful sailor and another man, armed with axes.

"There's no one to man the fire now," said the sailor. "Will they bring us in, or let us die?"

"They can't get to us till the fire in the water dies down, and by then we'll be dead meat," said the other.

Harry gulped. The only answer was for him to man the nozzle. "I'll do it. I'll point the fire."

The boat rocked violently as the angry serpent burst out of the water again. To their relief no more heads had grown. They had just two to deal with.

"Now!" cried one of the sailors. "Now's our chance!" The sailors struck together. Both heads fell at once. Which should Harry attack with the flame first? He turned the nozzle to the left and the stump withered away. One stump was left now, but as Harry turned, the flame fizzled. Disaster! Harry saw the end of the stump beginning to swell, like a plant budding. If three more heads emerged on the Hydra, everything would be over.

There must be a blockage in the pipe. Harry looked around for something to clear it and saw a paddle on the floor. He picked it up and whacked the nozzle. Fire flowed again and he pointed it at the last head, but not before the nozzle spurted and spat fire onto Harry's hand.

The flames crawled up his arm like flesh-eating insects, devouring his skin. Harry did not see the headless monster sink into the sea. He only felt the pain of the fire. He collapsed onto the floor of the boat, screaming and screaming, oblivious to anything else.

More than half an hour passed while the fire subsided around the boat. The talkative sailor wrapped Harry's arm in cloth to extinguish the flame. The sailors had brightened up a bit, talking to each other about the freedom they had won through their battle with the monster, discussing how they would become famous for their exploits. Harry heard some of this, his headed cushioned only by the wooden thwarts, as he passed in and out of consciousness on the floor of the boat.

Eventually, the flames on the water subsided enough for the boat to reach the harbour wall again. The soothsayer stood calmly with a group of soldiers. Harry was carried like a dead weight on the shoulder of the cheerful sailor and laid carefully on the quay.

The volunteers expected to be congratulated and applauded, but instead they were each grabbed by two soldiers. The soothsayer simply looked at them and said, "Take them away."

"But we're free now! It was a promise!" shouted the cheerful sailor. The response he had was a crack on the head with a sword-hilt from one of the soldiers. He slumped, semi-conscious. The soothsayer looked at them, more cruel and more dictatorial than the man he served. "Caesar does not tolerate men who fail in their duty. He is busy and now on his way to defeat his human enemies. Your have won you freedom. But your freedom will not be in this world. It will be in the next. Take them away - and let them speak to no one else."

Harry listened to this from afar, wondering what his own fate would be when the promises to these men were so easily broken. Then he passed out completely.

19. A Plan

After Harry had been thrown into the boat, Neos was marched back to the Palace with instructions that he was not to leave his own rooms and should be guarded at all times.

Neos had no intention of staying in his bedroom under house arrest. As soon as he arrived, he made plans to leave again without anyone noticing. It would not be the first time. He pushed a piece of furniture in front of his door so no one could enter. He decided against climbing out of the window and edging himself around the parapet. He was too likely to be spotted with so many people around during the siege. Instead he opened up a metal grate in the corner of the room. This was an access to the hypocaust system - the underfloor heating. Alexandria was rarely cold, but his rooms were among those connected to the heating system for occasional use in the winter. Months before, Neos had eased the grate open and explored underneath most of the main rooms in the Library and Palace. There was a gap of about half a metre he could crawl through and he knew the other exits and entry points. It was a secret route around the Palace whenever he wanted.

Slipping on his stomach into the hypocaust, he began to explore.

Eleanor was still in Nicomachus's study. They were unaware of what was going on elsewhere and of Harry's adventures in the harbour. Nicomachus had fallen into a momentary silence after his realisation that the magic of the Scroll itself might have brought the children into the Library of Alexandria from the future.

"What I fear most is fire," said Nicomachus. "I keep having visions of fire, not just the explosion we witnessed earlier. For all my long life, the Scroll has been in the safest place I know, lying at rest with Alexander, the man to whom I gave my first life and to whom I gave my oath to protect the book. Now I am not sure. But perhaps there is a way - with your help."

Nicomachus stood up more nimbly than a four-hundred-year-old man had a right to do. He reached up to the highest shelves and pulled down a large scroll. Dust had settled on the top and Nicomachus blew it off. The dust tickled Eleanor's nose as he passed her the scroll. Then he went to the table and picked up a small ivory box which he put into a satchel that he hung around his neck.

"Go on. Unroll the Scroll."

"Is it the same as the one in Alexander's tomb?" asked Eleanor with some surprise.

"Not quite."

"No," said Eleanor looking at the picture of the Hydra, happily ignorant that Harry was tackling a real one outside the building. She twisted her hair as she studied the Scroll.

"The writing is all rubbish."

"Exactly. In the many years I have been in this temple, I have considered how I might best protect the Scroll. This was one of my early projects, almost forgotten, but now it may be useful. I made a copy. It took years for me to master the ability to draw this. There were few others I could trust and they are all gone now, but in the end I managed to make a good copy. But the words are rubbish - deliberately. They are just pretty pictures. But tell me, how did you and your friend..."

"Brother," Eleanor corrected him.

"Ah, brother then. How did you manage to read the words? I don't know anyone else who has ever been able to do so. I know them off by heart but four hundred years is a long time to learn something, and even then I had magic at my disposal to help translate. But you and your brother. How did you do it?"

Eleanor wished she could tell him, but she didn't understand it herself. "I just can." It was something she and Harry had just been able to do. The strange thing was that when she had looked at the words with Harry in the book in the tomb, they didn't appear to make any sense. The characters weren't even familiar. She couldn't have said, "That's an 'e' or that's a 'z'." She just knew what they meant.

Nicomachus looked at her kindly. "There is magic in this world that we can never understand. It is too mysterious for us, too rooted in the depths of time and imbued with the power of the gods."

There was a scuffling, some sort of movement. Eleanor looked up. "What's that? Did you hear that noise?"

They listened again carefully, but there was nothing.

"No. I expect it's just rats. They creep about under the floor sometimes at this time of year. Nothing to worry about."

"Rats? Yuk!" Eleanor leapt to her feet, but Nicomachus ignored her.

"I have an idea, but there is no way I can carry it out on my own," said Nicomachus. "We must exchange the Scroll in Alexander's tomb for this one. It is no longer secure now that

Caesar and Cleopatra have access. We must replace it with this copy and then hide the genuine one or carry it away to safety."

"How? Is there someone who can help?"

"Yes. You." The old man sighed sadly. "There were others, but they are all gone. Others like me, bound by Alexander's oath to protect the book, although theirs was only a short lifetime's commitment. When the rumours that Cleopatra's brother was using some of the lesser scrolls to bring monsters up from The Nether World began, Caesar and Cleopatra started to look for magical ways to counter him. That was when they broke the sanctity of this Library. They tortured my colleagues, and one by one they all succumbed and told part of the story. But I am the only one who knows the whole truth."

"So why didn't they torture you too?"

"I was the last. The 'secret librarian' as I was known to my brothers. I had not been outside the temple and Library in two hundred years. Only the other librarians knew of my existence until recently. And then they found me. I knew they would and I knew they would come for me. I was not ready to destroy the book or myself, so I told Caesar and Cleopatra that I would help them. My power would be the one to unlock the dark secrets of the book. But I lied. I am ashamed of it as I have spent so long speaking only the truth, but it was the only way. I offered to help if they would reward me with my freedom and power of my own. They are so power-hungry they believed others must be too. But then the siege began in earnest, and you and your brother arrived in the tomb. There has not been time for them to disprove my lie. Now there is hope. You."

"But how can I help?"

"The main entrance to the tomb is guarded and can be accessed only in the company of Caesar himself. Even I cannot gain access any more. But there is another way in, a way that has never been used and, even if it is guessed, is well protected."

Eleanor was thinking quickly as she listened. She was remembering the tomb, when she watched the Phoenix circle around inside it and then leave. "From above," she said.

"Yes. From above. In the pool there is what appears to be a well-head which provides fresh air to the mausoleum. It is so small that only a child can squeeze through. But you could be lowered down on a rope to exchange the real book for the copy. After that we must organise your escape to your own time. You must become a guardian of the Scroll and protect it. My time for rest will come. I must face my destiny with Caesar."

Eleanor wasn't ready to accept this sort of responsibility. Quite apart from the fact that she didn't like heights, she wasn't going to leave and escape without Harry - or Grace, who must also be here somewhere.

"I won't leave them behind!" she shouted out without explaining. "And I won't do it without them!" She put her head in her hands and sobbed. "I just want to go home!"

Nicomachus was at a loss as to what to do. Four hundred years had taught him nothing about children. After further thought, he held out his hand.

"Come with me," he said. "We will go and find Hypatia. She will help, and she is the only one we can trust. Shall we?"

He led her out of the room and down a corridor towards a different part of the building.

As they left the room, Neos stretched out from his hiding place underneath the floor. He thought he had been caught when Eleanor heard him, and had laughed at the explanation about rats. In spite of cramp in his legs, he had remained absolutely quiet, even when rats actually ran over his legs. What he had heard was far too interesting. This, he thought to himself, would be his route to power and his route to revenge against Caesar for the way he was treated. He would have the Scroll for himself and then the world would be his to command.

20. Disguise

"I found her running away from Neos, Mama," said Kasya, taking it for granted that anyone running away from Neos deserved looking after. She had brought Grace to the Palace kitchens, knowing that Hypatia would be there somewhere and they had a chance of being alone, as it was not yet time to prepare the evening meal.

Kasya's mother looked at Grace, then turned her head away, anxious not to be thought to be rude by staring. Grace liked the look of her and said simply, "I'm Grace."

"Welcome, Grace. I am Hypatia. Shall we be friends?" Grace nodded. Hypatia took a step towards her. "May I?" she asked as she put her hand out to touch Grace's hair. "Yellow hair is rare in Alexandria. As for blue eyes, they are even more unusual. You must be hidden. The trouble is that although we might hide you in the Palace or the Library, there are so few people in Alexandria who look like you, whoever does see you will instantly talk about you. That's quite apart from the dog."

"Sophie is her name."

"Sophie, yes, she is charming, but no one will have ever seen a dog like this either. Sophie must stay out of sight. Ah, I have an idea. We must disguise you. And then as long as you look down with your eyes, perhaps you will not be recognized. But you should cast your eyes down anyway. A girl of your age should not look at adults at all." Grace dropped her eyes quickly.

Hypatia laughed. "Not me. You can look at me!"

"See?" Kasya said to Grace, "I told you she'd be helpful. She's my friend as well as my mother." Grace smiled rather mistily, wishing she had a mother like Hypatia. Kasya squeezed her hand in sympathy.

"Kasya," said Hypatia. "Go and get me some walnut oil from the kitchen stores and then run to the garden and gather up some henna. Quickly as you can. And you, Grace, when did you last eat?"

"Er - this morning," said Grace.

"Then you must be hungry - and Sophie too. While we wait for Kasya, let me see what I can do."

Hypatia found some scraps of meat for Sophie and gave Grace a stew of chickpeas and onions flavoured with herbs, and some heavy brown bread to eat with it. The stew was delicious. There was also a beaker of milk, which tasted strange to her.

"You don't like it? It's the very best asses' milk. Good for you," said Hypatia. "Our Queen takes so much of it they say she bathes in it!"

After the chickpea stew came dates, dark brown and sticky, like the walnut oil which Kasya returned with. Hypatia opened the stopper carefully. "This is very expensive. I think the Queen would be furious if she knew what I was using it for. But it stains well, as I have learnt from spilling it on my hands. Have you finished?" she asked Grace, who hastily swallowed the last date. "Lean back now, and shut your eyes - tightly, but not squeezed." Hypatia dabbed a cloth with the oil and smoothed it all over Grace's face. A little dribbled down the side of her nose and she said, "It tickles."

"Mouth shut, please," said Hypatia adding more oil to the side of Grace's mouth. "There. It's done. Your face is finished. No more pale white skin to give you away. It's not as dark as our skin, but since you're going to end up looking like a little rich girl who keeps out of the sun, that doesn't matter at all."

The next task was to do her hair. The plant Kasya had collected from the garden was now all crushed into a green paste in a bowl in front of them. Hypatia mixed it with water and soon it was a revolting clay-like mud.

"You're not going to make my hair green are you?"

"No," laughed Hypatia. "This looks green now, but will make your hair go a deep red!"

"I think that's worse!" replied Grace.

"Not as bad as this though; I need to cut your hair."

"Do you really?" asked Grace, more shocked about the idea of losing her long locks than the idea of becoming a redhead. She was proud of her long blonde hair. It had taken years to grow.

"I am afraid you must. It's all the fashion and if you didn't, it would look out of place. May I?"

Grace nodded uncertainly. Hypatia looked at her gently, holding her hand. "I promise it will look good. I'm good at cutting hair, aren't I Kasya? But try not to cry. I don't want tears creating streaky marks down the side of your nice new brown face!"

Grace tried to be brave and Sophie lay across her feet in sympathy to keep her company. Hypatia cut Grace's hair into a crisp bob.

"Can I see?" asked Grace.

"Not yet," said Hypatia, teasing. "We'll wait until it's dyed. Then you'll see the full effect."

Grace's hair was coated in the disgusting clay mix, which was eventually washed out, and Hypatia rubbed Grace's head with a linen towel.

"Now, Kasya, fetch a mirror!"

Grace was shocked. She simply didn't recognise herself. Her hair was a deep carrot red and in such a different style that she didn't know who she looked like. She stared at herself for a minute or two and then decided that if she had to be disguised, there were worse ways of doing it.

"You look wonderful and if not entirely Egyptian, no one would notice at first glance. I think even Neos would find it difficult to recognise you," said Kasya.

Grace still felt a little forlorn but she managed a quick, "Thank you," to Hypatia. When Hypatia told her that she also looked several years older, she decided that maybe it really was worth losing all that hair for.

Sophie heard the noise first, her ears pricked up. She gave the softest of barks. Then they all heard footsteps coming down the corridor towards the kitchens. Grace whispered, "Where should I hide?" Kasya jumped up and opened a doorway that led into a large storeroom full of amphorae and other pots. Sophie was too well-bred and intelligent a dog to need to be told to follow or remain quiet. The main door into the kitchen swung open and in walked Nicomachus and Eleanor.

Kasya shyly took a step back and looked at the floor. She was in awe of this man. Even the child slaves of the Palace knew he was privy to the secrets of Caesar and Cleopatra. Hypatia's reaction was quite different. She broke into a smile and greeted Nicomachus warmly.

"Come and meet Nicomachus, Kasya." Kasya was confused and it showed in her face. As a slave, she knew her mother belonged to Cleopatra, but she also knew that her mother had little respect for her owner. Yet here she was welcoming one of the Queen's confidants like a long-lost friend. More than that, Nicomachus moved to Hypatia and held both her hands in his own, a sure sign of comfort and trust.

"Come and greet Nico, Kasya. It's all right. He is a friend, and more than a friend: the very best of friends. Whatever you have heard about him over the last few weeks, we can trust him. I assure you of that."

Kasya trusted her mother absolutely, but even she was inclined to doubt this. It was so different to everything she had heard about what had been going on in the Library. But when she looked up she saw Eleanor, and gasped. The long blonde hair. The blue eyes. This was a girl who looked just like her new friend Grace. In her astonishment, Kasya forgot all her manners and just stared.

"Kasya!" Her mother's stern words broke her from her trance.

"Do not worry!" said Nicomachus, smiling. "I have heard a lot about you, Kasya. It is a pleasure to meet you. But tell me, why do you look as if you have seen a ghost?"

"I don't know," said Kasya, still doubtful about sharing anything with this man.

"It's all right," said Hypatia, laughing. "You can let them out. Our secret is safe and perhaps Nicomachus can help."

"I fear it is the other way round," said Nicomachus, but at that moment Kasya opened the door to the store and beckoned Grace and Sophie out.

Sophie bounded across the room, more like a puppy than a full-grown dog. She licked Eleanor's face and Eleanor responded by dropping to her knees and hugging her tightly. "How did you get here, Sophie? It's so good to see you."

Wanting to tell her, but of course unable to speak, Sophie turned toward the red-headed girl. Eleanor stared. There was something familiar about the girl, but she couldn't make it out.

Grace said crossly, "Well, hello to you too."

"Grace?" asked Eleanor, still uncertain. Grace shook her bobbed hair, unused to its being so light and said, "Yes!"

Eleanor ran over and hugged her cousin. Hypatia laughed. "I guess our disguise works well enough."

Nicomachus coughed politely, interrupting them. "We have very little time." So, after some hasty interruptions and without waiting to hear just how Grace had come to be in Alexandria too (he made it clear that could wait for another time) he explained in a few succinct sentences just what they needed to do.

"Access to the top of Alexander's tomb can only be reached by a child. The opening is far too small for an adult. And the worry is that it is a long way to climb down a rope."

"That's OK," said Eleanor. "Grace is a really good climber. She's sure to be able to manage. She's always climbing trees and things at home."

Grace wasn't quite sure about being volunteered like this, but she was also proud at being admired for her gymnastic achievements, especially from her cousin who wasn't always the first to praise her.

"There is another problem too, which I haven't mentioned yet. It's the location of the opening into the tomb," said Nicomachus. He turned to Eleanor and continued gravely, "You have already seen it. It's in the centre of the pool where the sacred crocodiles live. And we have no time to lose. The crocodiles will be hungry again soon."

If Grace's skin hadn't been stained dark with the walnut oil, they would all have noticed that she had turned pale. "Thanks a lot!" she whispered sharply and sarcastically to Eleanor.

21. Swapping the Scroll

In the great hallway of the Library, Grace looked for the first time at the dark square pool of water, completely still and mirror-like.

"It doesn't look so dangerous now," she said nervously.

"It'll be fine," said Eleanor, not even beginning to convince herself.

During the siege the Library was virtually empty. They had avoided running into anyone on the way to the pool by way of a workmen's store where they had found some long lengths of rope.

Sophie stood at the edge of the pond staring into the deep waters below, her nose nearly touching the water, sniffing it carefully and inspecting the edges.

"Under no circumstances must you let anything drop into or touch the pond," said Nicomachus. Sophie swiftly lifted her nose away from the water as if she'd suddenly been warned it was poisonous. "The crocodiles will still be sleepy from their last feed, but they are also looking forward to their next. If we touch the water it will wake them and stir them up. Then it will be much more difficult."

Grace shuddered. Eleanor saw the shudder and said, "I don't know why I said it'll be fine. It won't be. We can't do this."

Nicomachus had seen the shudder too. "We should think again," he agreed. "I can't send you down."

"But you told Eleanor there wasn't another way."

"There isn't."

"It's too dangerous," added Eleanor. She was begging now. "Don't do it!"

Grace felt braver. She shrugged her shoulders. "It's like a dare. I'm sure I can manage. Let's go!"

Many visitors to the Library of Alexandria had commented on the charm of the pool and the little well in its centre, but that was in the sunlight. Now, in the dark, lit only by the lamps, the black water looked sinister. There was a small circular wall on top of the 'wellhead', which Grace would have to squeeze through.

"Here is my idea," said Nicomachus. "We will stretch one rope across the pool from one side to the other. We can tie it to the balustrade that surrounds the little gallery above us. Then Grace will have to cross it, carrying the longer rope, before dropping that one down the well to the altar below. It's a long way down. Can you manage that?" he asked Grace.

Grace looked around at the little balustrade, judging the distances. She could do it. She nodded.

"Good. Then let's waste no more time." There was a convincing energy in the way Nicomachus was leading them. After centuries as a librarian, his old leadership skills from his time as a warrior with Alexander the Great came back easily. He gave energy to the enterprise and they all felt they would achieve what they set out to do.

Nicomachus took one end of the rope and attached it to the balcony. Then they walked round the gallery until they were immediately opposite where they'd started from, so that the rope stretched over the top of the 'wellhead' in the centre. Nicomachus made the other end fast to the balustrade.

He looped another rope over Grace's shoulder and tied a

knot from one end of this to the rope stretched horizontally across the water, so that it could slide. "When you first put your weight on the second rope, this one will sag, but do not worry. Keep going. It will hold."

Finally, he took a satchel from his shoulder and gave it to Grace. "This contains the copy of the Scroll. The other will be on top of Alexander's tomb - it's like a large table. Change them round and climb back up. Remember, when climbing down the rope, put one hand over the other or you will slide and lose the skin off your hands."

If Grace hadn't been so nervous, she might have taken offence at being told such a basic thing about climbing ropes, but she just nodded.

"Go now then, before you think too much about what you are doing. And don't look down!"

As Grace crept along the rope moving hand over hand, Nicomachus turned to the others. "There is little hope if she does fall into the pool, but gather up anything to throw into the water if she does - the little lamps all around the side will do. That might just distract them for long enough."

Eleanor and Sophie didn't wait to be told twice, nor did Kasya and Hypatia. They watched as Grace reached the wellhead and began to lower the second rope down into the tomb. Eleanor was partly anxious, partly jealous at how easy Grace made it look. All they could do now was wait as she vanished into the tomb.

Grace had been afraid that she would have to lower herself into darkness, but the sides of the 'well' gave off a dim luminous glow that helped her to see where she was going. Hand over hand she went, then suddenly, her feet lost their grip.

The rope was too short.

She dangled for a moment, her whole body-weight held by

her hands, before her feet found the rope again. Then she paused, catching her breath and looked down. Dark, glowing eyes looked up at her. Grace gasped. Someone was in the room below, looking up at her! But the eyes didn't move, and Grace let out a breath of relief. Of course! The sarcophagus was painted with figures - and there was the Scroll, lying on top of it.

As her feet touched the tomb, she was about to let go of the rope, but she felt it pulling back at her. The top of the rope was not fixed to something solid. It was fixed to the other rope. As soon as she let go, it would pull back out of reach and she would be stuck.

The muscles in her arms were agony. What if she let go? She would be trapped and die of starvation. That thought gave her enough strength for another effort. She pulled herself higher up the rope and clamped her feet around it. So far, so good. Then clinging by one hand, she let go with the other and tied the rope around her ankle. That would keep her safe. If only she'd had an audience to see. She dropped down headfirst and all the blood rushed to her head, making her feel giddy. But her feet held. It worked!

She could just reach the Scroll. She replaced it with the copy, and then twisted upright again for the long climb back to the top. The climb seemed endless, and she was getting cold, apart from her hands, which burned like fire. The muscles in her legs were aching and the rope had made a sore on her ankle.

When she emerged from the wellhead Nicomachus and Eleanor hugged each other. Tears were running down Eleanor's face. Sophie's tail thumped.

"Well done!" Nicomachus said.

But as Grace climbed back over the balcony, the satchel swung against the side. The Scroll slipped out. It bounced on the edge and fell into the pool. Sophie leapt in after it.

The crocodiles surfaced.

Eleanor and Nicomachus threw their lamps into the pool, but what good it would do? The crocodiles were surging toward them and Sophie was in the water, seconds away from becoming the crocodiles' next meal. The crocodiles were after her, lashing their huge tails. They were much faster than the dog, but had further to go. The placid water turned into foam. Waves washed across the floor. "Go, Sophie go!" screamed Grace in agony. None of them could reach Sophie in time.

Then the crocodiles were denied their dinner as Sophie was yanked from the pool by someone else. The graceful deerhound spluttered and dropped the Scroll on the floor. Recovering and shaking herself, Sophie bent to pick up the Scroll in her gentle mouth again, but it was snatched away from her.

Neos had appeared out of nowhere. He picked up the Scroll and looked at the horrified group. "Just what I want. And just what you slaves are for: to do my dirty work." Then before anyone could react or move, he ran off down the corridor of the library, saying, "I doubt your friend Harry survived that fire in the harbour. I expect it was a painful death."

22. Recapture

Grace lay slumped against one of the tall columns, withdrawn into herself, inconsolable. The Scroll was gone, and it sounded as though Harry was gone too. Sophie was tearing down the corridor after Neos with Eleanor close behind. What was the point? They'd never catch him. All their efforts had been for nothing.

Then Nicomachus commanded, "No! Wait! Come back!"

Eleanor and the dog stopped running.

Nicomachus was undoing the knots on the ropes. Then he looped them carefully over his shoulder as Eleanor came back, furious. She was so angry that she pummelled Nicomachus's arm.

"Why did you stop me chasing him? We might have been able to catch him."

"There is no way you could have caught the boy without being arrested by the guards. This way we have a chance, however small." Eleanor stopped hitting him and looked up. Although his words were firm and strong, she saw that he looked sad and hopeless. She buried her face in his sleeve, realising that he felt their failure as much as she and Grace - or more. The Scroll was in his charge. He had lost it.

"We can't stay here. The keepers will come soon to feed the

beasts. We must return to the kitchens. No one will be there at this time of night."

They put back the ropes where they belonged and went down to the kitchens. Hypatia and Kasya had been waiting for them, and gave them cool water to drink, and lumps of fresh-baked bread, which put a little heart into Eleanor and Grace.

"There is something about that boy Neos which troubles me more than the combined armies of Caesar and Cleopatra," said Nicomachus. "I cannot read him at all. He is blocked from my vision - always has been. But we must be as optimistic as we can. Thanks to Grace, the Scroll has been changed over and still none of us have been arrested or stopped."

Kasya interrupted, "But won't Neos just run and take the Scroll to Caesar for him to use?"

"He may," said Nicomachus, "in which case all is lost, but he may not. I think we must not underestimate how devious Neos is - or how self-centred. He wants the Scroll for himself. He hates Caesar. In the meantime, we must continue as we were to avoid suspicion. This means that you, Eleanor, must be brave and return to the dungeon with me. If I am not arrested, we will know that we are not betrayed yet. Grace must continue to hide in her disguise. And we must make plans to follow the real - and the false - scrolls on their journeys."

Grace looked mutinous and Eleanor's heart sank at the thought of the dungeon again, but neither of them had any time to voice their thoughts. They could hear the tramp of soldiers' feet approaching. Had Nicomachus been wrong about Neos?

"It's the Palace Guard!" said Hypatia. "Hide!"

"Only Grace and Sophie must hide. Go with them, Kasya. To the store-room, quick!" commanded Nicomachus quietly, gripping Eleanor's arm. The grip was tight and unfriendly. "I'm sorry," he whispered, "We're going to have to play this out. You are my prisoner in front of these guards. They exaggerate the cruelty they believe their master expects and they enjoy seeing it in others."

There was no time for Eleanor to complain. The doors were thrown open and four Roman soldiers marched in. One of them had something on his shoulder covered in a cloth. It was a body - a small body.

"Where is Hypatia? She is needed," said the guard.

Hypatia came forward and bowed to the soldier. By rank she was a mere slave, but her importance as Cleopatra's head slave and personal attendant outweighed her slave status. The soldier and Hypatia looked at each other, aware of these differences.

"It is Caesar's order that this boy is treated and returned to the dungeon in my care. We will wait."

Pots and pans clattered on the floor and smashed as two of the soldiers swept everything off the kitchen table. The body was dumped down. It groaned and the cloth covering the body fell to the floor. "Harry!" cried Eleanor, struggling to get to the table, but Nicomachus tightened his grip.

"Ow!' cried Eleanor. 'That hurts!"

Nicomachus drew back his hand to slap her across the face. She flinched, but his hand did not connect. Instead, Nicomachus smacked his own shoulder. The sound was enough to be convincing. The guard turned towards the noise and saw the old man and Eleanor for the first time.

"What are you doing here?" he asked sternly. 'The Queen gave me clear orders to return both these foreign children to the dungeon as soon as Hypatia has treated the boy.

"I came for herbs for truth potions that I need," Nicomachus answered quickly. "Now, thanks to you, they are crushed on the floor." He indicated the heap of pots. 'Hypatia will have to find me fresh ones."

"Yes," said Hypatia. 'You are a hindrance. I need space. Withdraw. Outside."

The soldier hesitated. Hypatia repeated, "Withdraw now."

"Very well. I will remain with the guards outside."

"As you wish," replied Hypatia, ignoring him.

As the doors closed behind the soldiers, Nicomachus released Eleanor from his grip and she rushed to Harry. His breathing was short and painful from the fumes he had inhaled. She was about to put her hand on his arm when she saw the burn, red, blistered and oozing onto the table. Harry opened his eyes and smiled. "We killed the Hydra."

"I need Kasya," interrupted Hypatia. She called, and Kasya came out of the store-room, Grace and Sophie with her. Harry looked woozily at the two girls, then opened his eyes wider as he recognized his cousin underneath her new red hair, "Grace?"

"Yes."

Harry looked as if he would like to ask a question, but closed his eyes instead. Sophie laid her head on the table beside him and licked his cheek. Hypatia made a poultice of herbs and some sort of fat and gently applied it to Harry's burn. The two girls looked at him.

"At least we're together again. That's a relief."

"Is he your brother?" asked Kasya, who was holding Hypatia's salves.

"He's Eleanor's brother," replied Grace. "He's my cousin."

They all felt much better for being reunited. Harry and Eleanor looked at each other, then Eleanor remembered there was something she had to say. "I'm sorry I blamed you for everything before."

"It's OK."

Nicomachus spoilt the reunion. "You have only a few moments together while Hypatia treats these wounds. We must catch up and plan the parts we need to play in the days ahead."

"I thought it was all over just then when the Palace guard showed up," said Grace.

So the children told each other about their adventures while Kasya and Hypatia fussed over Harry, tending to his wounds and making him drink a deep herbal potion which Hypatia said would help him sleep and recover from the pain.

Then came the dread noise they had been fearing. The measured tread of more soldiers' feet along the hall outside the kitchen. It was enough notice for Grace and Sophie to vanish into hiding in the storeroom again, but not enough for the children to say goodbye to each other.

Then the doors were flung open.

Cleopatra stood before them. All Hypatia's previous confidence in the presence of armed soldiers now evaporated. Cleopatra's arrival was like a whirlwind, her presence dominating all else. Beside her was the cat, elegant but with just enough of its sabre teeth showing to look menacing. The Queen's personal bodyguard marched into the kitchen and formed up all around the room, alert and protective.

Cleopatra's presence in the kitchens was unprecedented. Kasya was nearly guilty of staring - a serious offence - but just in time she cast down her eyes to the floor as her mother had always taught her.

Only now did Cleopatra move into the room, and look at the body lying on the table. Harry had seen the Queen arrive and sensibly shut his eyes, playing dead. She surveyed the mess on the floor where the soldiers had swept the table clear of its pots and pans. She sensed Nicomachus and Eleanor behind her and turned to inspect them, as if they were pieces of unwanted furniture. No one spoke. No one would dare speak to Cleopatra unless they were asked a question first.

"I am glad I have never been to the kitchens if this is the way they are kept."

The silence continued while the Queen inspected the rest of the room. She spent a long time staring at the storeroom as if aware there was something in there that shouldn't be. Then she looked at the body again. And at Eleanor.

"This is the second time I have seen these foreign wizards in a place they should not be. They should both be in the dungeons."

It was not a question but a statement.

"However," said the Queen, "they will not return to the dungeons. They will come to Rome. Their fate will be decided there. Hypatia, your job is to keep that boy alive.

"We leave at dawn. You will prepare my household to depart in Caesar's flagship. Caesar has won a great victory outside Alexandria against my brother Ptolemy. Upper and Lower Egypt are mine again. But there is pressing business in Rome. Tomorrow at dawn. You will be ready."

Hypatia bowed low. "It shall be done, my lady."

Cleopatra looked at the children again. "The household guard will remain with you." Turning to the guards and indicating Harry, she said, "You will not let this boy out of your sight. Understand?"

As if to emphasise the point the cat extended its sabre teeth to their full extent.

"Yes, my lady," said the guards' leader, bowing low.

"Yes, my lady," said Hypatia, also bowing.

"Librarian," added Cleopatra, turning towards Nicomachus. "You will come with me. Bring the girl. Caesar has need of you and we have work to do."

Nicomachus relaxed his grip from Eleanor's arm and bowed.

One of the guards had a collar and a lead in his hand. Had they spotted Sophie? Were they going to take her? Then the guard came over to Eleanor. He pulled her long ponytail upwards, and fastened the collar around her neck. She was to be treated like an animal!

Cleopatra left the room, followed by Nicomachus, Eleanor and some of the guards. The remaining guards stayed with Hypatia, Kasya and Harry. Grace and Sophie had to stay hidden in their cupboard. The children were split up again.

There was no way out.

23. Arson

Once again, Eleanor was standing in front of the tomb of Alexander. Her fingers tried to loosen the collar around her neck, but it was too tight to stretch. Nicomachus, Cleopatra, Caesar and his soothsayer were gathered together. This time a troop of soldiers accompanied the group. For four hundred years, underneath the famous Library of Alexandria, the tomb of Alexander the Great and the secret hiding-place of the ancient Scroll had only been visited by those sworn to safeguard its secrets. Now it was invaded. Nicomachus was shivering, not from cold, but from fear that he had been mistaken in trying to preserve the Scroll rather than destroy it.

Caesar was triumphant. The siege of Alexandria was over. Egypt was his. The Scroll was his, though his military victory had proved the magicians were not needed. Even Cleopatra was his. He would return to Rome and Rome would be his, another triumph. The Senate of Rome would bow before him. Rome would no longer be a republic, but a kingdom and he would be king - and not just a king, but an emperor.

"Take the Scroll, Librarian. We go to Rome now. Its secrets can be unravelled there, if necessary."

But for the events of the last few hours, this would have been Nicomachus's last stand. He would have defied Caesar and

Cleopatra. He would have stood firm and stayed committed to his last vow to Alexander. He would have destroyed the Scroll and accepted the consequences. But of course he knew it was a fake. Obediently he picked up the forgery from the tomb and walked back towards the stairs, standing tall. This should have been a moment of absolute shame, but instead there was a spark of hope. Neos had proved himself to be as devious as expected: he had kept the theft of the Scroll to himself.

Caesar led the group from the tomb at a swift march. Eleanor was dragged through unfamiliar passageways, gasping as the collar pulled at her neck. The oily smoke of guttering lamps in alcoves along the passageway made her cough more. Then they entered the copying-room she had seen earlier.

Caesar stopped abruptly and raised his hand in command for everyone else to do the same. He lifted his foot and Eleanor saw a sticky fluid drip from the sole of his sandal back to floor. There was a puddle of something, too thick to be water. It was like glue. Caesar was about to touch it when he hesitated and squatted down instead, his toga dropping onto the floor into the puddle. The sticky stuff snaked between the low desks and through a door to another part of the library. Caesar sniffed carefully like a dog and then stood agâin.

"No one must move! Silence!" he commanded.

Eleanor saw him draw a dagger from his toga. He turned it on himself. He cut the toga well above the hem and tore it to the floor. Then carefully he stepped out of his sandals and moved back to the group behind him, stepping over the puddle.

"By all the gods! Greek Fire!" he said, and his tanned face was pale. "Do not tread in it! It must be stopped. The criminal cannot have gone far. Where does that trail lead, Librarian?"

"That is the storeroom, sir, full of blank papyrus ready for copying," answered Nicomachus. He too was pale with horror. "Then it leads towards the main library."

"It is deadly! What heathen would do this?" demanded Caesar.

A crash broke the silence and a small cauldron rolled across the door of the storeroom, spilling what was left of the contents. Then they heard running footsteps.

"You, and you, go after him!" shouted Caesar, turning to his soldiers. "Catch him or kill him, I do not care which!"

They ran. One soldier got through the door, but the second one slipped on an unseen puddle. Skidding across the floor, he grabbed for the door-frame, but misjudged it and fell with a thump. His helmet hit the floor and rang out like a bell. The metal scraped on the stone floor. The friction caused a single spark to shoot from the helmet, straight to the trail of fluid. There was a whoosh and an evil snake of flame writhed across the floor towards them.

"Out of the building, now!" cried Caesar.

They raced across the room. The silence of the library was broken by the crackling of dry material as centuries of scholarship was reduced to ashes. The fire leapt from floor to ceiling, the flames fed with warm air from outside, growing higher and higher. Papyrus crackled and exploded. As bookshelves collapsed in flames, the next stack was hungry for destruction. Eleanor felt the heat warm her face.

They ran past the crocodile pool, then into the open. As they turned to look back, an explosion tore through the centre of the building and flames roared through the columns of the great temple to knowledge and wisdom.

Eleanor saw proud Alexandrians rush to form chains of men, women and children with buckets of water. They began to form lines from the harbour and from the Nile to quench the flames.

"It will do no good," said Caesar.

Nicomachus had tears in his eyes. He too knew it would do no good. Greek fire! Each bucket of water only added to the inferno. The greatest repository of knowledge in the world was being destroyed before their eyes. Cleopatra was openly weeping.

"Come, my love," said Caesar, putting his arm round the Queen. He seemed to have forgotten his strange appearance, barefoot with a torn toga. "Our ship - and our destiny - awaits us."

Cleopatra stared. "But - how can we go to Rome now?" She gestured to the burning Library.

"It has perished," said Caesar. "We can do nothing."

"Can nothing be saved? Who can have done this?"

"I promise you," said Caesar, between his teeth, "that I will find the culprit and when I have finished with him he will wish he too had perished in the fire he set. Come, let us go."

Even the human chain of fire-fighters made way for the Royal party as it followed Caesar and the Queen to the harbour to board Caesar's galley. As soon as they were aboard, the deck crew cast off and the slave rowers took up their oars, moving at battle speed out of reach of the flames.

Nicomachus stood at the stern of the boat, looking back at Alexandria and his Library, aflame. The tears streamed down his face unceasingly. The famous lighthouse was insignificant compared to the burning Library. Now Eleanor knew why his foresight had seen only fire.

At the other end of the galley, in the bow, she saw Neos leaning back and watching the flames. He looked smug and contented. She wondered why.

Then a soldier pulled on the lead around her neck and took her below to join Harry, already locked up. Where were Grace and Sophie?

Was there any hope left after all these disasters?

24. Departing for Rome

As Nicomachus left the kitchens, Grace stood behind the door. She heard everything said by Cleopatra. She knew that Rome was a long sea journey away. She sat down and stroked Sophie's soft ears, thinking.

She had to get on the same boat as Harry and Eleanor. But how? She knew she could get out of the Palace and Library complex through the secret entrance Neos had shown her earlier, but whether she could manage to be a stowaway on the Royal Galley was quite another matter. The other problem was Sophie. How could she possibly get the dog onto the boat without being seen?

The door opened a tiny crack, then a little more. Grace held her breath. Maybe this was it. Were they going to catch her? Someone slipped in and shut it.

"Grace?" came a whisper. It was Kasya.

"Are you going to Rome?" asked Grace.

"Yes."

"I need to come with you."

"Of course you must," said Kasya. "I just don't know how yet. I don't even know how to get you out of the Palace. It must be so heavily guarded now."

"I can do that," said Grace. "Neos brought me in through a

secret way."

"Well, that helps. There's someone else I want to find and take to Rome too. He's a Roman boy. He's one of the ones who came every day for bread when I brought you in here. I think he could be useful in Rome. He'll know his way around. I think you'll like him," Kasya added.

"What about his parents?" asked Grace. "Won't they miss him?"

"It's sad. They both died during the siege. He's an orphan. He doesn't have anyone. And I think he'll help."

"I'm an orphan too," said Grace. Kasya found her way towards Grace's voice in the darkness and it was the most natural thing to give her a hug, but they knew not to dwell on it now. It was too painful and there were too many other things to think about.

"If you can really get us out of the Palace," said Kasya, 'I think I can sort out Sophie and our friend. Give me a little time."

She left the room and Grace wondered what she was planning. There was silence for a while, and then she heard was Hypatia saying loudly, "I need all the Queen's slaves here at once. All of them, including the children."

It was clear one of the guards was arguing, but Hypatia was defiant. "Guarding these two children is your job, but you clearly have no idea how much baggage Her Majesty travels with. It usually takes a week to pack. Baggage will be coming and going all the time. Everyone must help."

From the sound of the footsteps rapidly moving around in the kitchen, Hypatia won her argument.

The storeroom door opened and two slaves dumped a large basket on the floor. The slaves went out, shutting the door behind them. Kasya climbed out of the basket.

"This is for Sophie," she said. The noble dog understood, but sniffed at the box a little reluctantly, before leaping in. There were blankets there to make her comfortable.

Grace gave the dog a kiss on the head. "See you in Rome." It was an unsatisfactory and hasty farewell and for a moment Grace wondered if they'd see each other again. She shook her head as if it could actually get rid of the gloomy thought.

With so many of the other child slaves in the rooms, the guards kept their eyes firmly on Harry. They could not pay attention to the other children wandering around the room as well. Kasya reappeared in the store-room.

"It's time," she whispered to Grace.

They heard Hypatia clap her hands. "Children! There's a basket in the storeroom. It needs to be carried carefully to go with the other luggage. Quickly now."

Some of the older, more muscular children opened the door and rushed into the storeroom. If they were surprised to find Kasya and Grace in there, they did not show it, especially when Kasya put her finger to her lips in the universal gesture of silence. They were used to being silent, used to being invisible. Eight of them carried the basket, Kasya and Grace included. Grace only just remembered to carry the bag she had been given in The Palace Library by Edgar and Jasper. As hoped, the guards paid them no attention. Then just as soon as they were outside the palace and near the garden with Neos's secret entrance, Kasya and Grace slipped away from the others with whispered thanks.

This time it was Grace's turn to take the lead. She ran straight to the bush against the main wall of the Palace and stepped behind it.

At first Kasya didn't realise how hiding behind a bush

could possibly help but as soon as Grace dropped down to her knees and began to crawl under the wall, Kasya understood. "I thought I knew every secret passage around this place. I guess I was wrong."

Once they were through and dusted down, Grace sniffed the air, "What's that smell? It's like incense."

"I don't know," replied Kasya. "It usually smells revolting out here - especially with all the rubbish with the siege. It's actually rather nice. But come on. Let's go."

It was Kasya's turn to lead, but suddenly they both jumped. A noise like a rumble of thunder came from behind the walls and an explosion lit up the sky, followed by an even stronger smell of incense. Even though the street had been busy, no one noticed the girls. There were vast numbers of people rushing past.

"The Library's on fire," they shouted. "We must help!"

"That's the smell. It's the papyrus in the Library burning! Quick!" said Kasya. "We must find Quintus, otherwise we will never track him down in this crowd. Keep up!"

She darted this way and that, hardly turning to check on Grace, who could only just keep up with her. They came to a large square with camels everywhere. Even the smell of smoke from the burning Library could not overcome the smell of the beasts. It was the camel market, normally sleepy and quiet at this time of day but now roused by the chaos of the burning library. Kasya didn't hesitate. She ran to one of the makeshift stalls and shouted, "Quintus! Quintus! Where are you?" Inside the stall she looked around at the blankets on the floor, kicking them. "Bother. He's gone."

"Who's gone?" said a voice behind her, making her jump.

"Quintus! You scared me."

"Ha!" said the boy boldly. He was in rags and was all skin and bone, but he had a big grin on his face.

"We need you, Quintus," Kasya said.

"So? What can I do that you can't get all those well-fed slave children to do?" He was smiling but Grace sensed there was a hint of bitterness behind what he was saying.

"Really, we need you, Quintus. In Rome."

"Rome? Home? But there's no home for me there any more than here now." His smile vanished. His face dropped. Kasya tried to touch him but he moved away.

"I'm going. We're going." Pointing to her companion, Kasya added, "This is Grace."

Quintus looked at them, covering up his sadness with well-practiced confidence. "You're really going to Rome aren't you?"

"Yes, we're really going."

He grinned cheekily. "Will there be food?"

Kasya smiled back, "Yes. There'll be food."

"Good. I'm in, then."

"We're going right now. Do you want to pack?"

Quintus stretched his arms out and made his grin even bigger, if possible. "I'm packed." He spun around. "This is all you get. I could pack some of that camel poo I use for bedding if you want. It's all around. Still sure you want me?"

"Yes," they laughed, "but without the poo!"

Quintus was slightly taller than the girls and walked between them, an arm round each of their shoulders.

"This," he said conspiratorially, "will be fun."

Grace wasn't quite sure what to make of him. He was so boisterous. But she liked him.

"Tell me," Quintus added, "how shall we get there. Shall we swim?"

It was Kasya's turn to grin. "I won't," she said grandly. "I shall travel with the Queen in her state apartments. You two will go in the bilge. Then we shall wash you off by dumping you overboard. You'll swim the last bit."

"You're joking!" said Quintus. "Aren't you?"

25. The Archers

In the chaos at the harbour, no one noticed Sophie's wet nose pressed against the outside of the basket she was hidden in. Except for Grace. Her own nose was tight up against Sophie's muzzle. She was so tightly squeezed against the side that the weave of the basket dug into her arms and made patterns. Worse, Quintus's feet were close to her face.

Kasya had managed to sneak them onto the dockside and shoved them into the basket abruptly. She sat on the top of it, holding the lid down, then rode it like a chariot as some of the slaves carried it into the boat.

In the darkness of the hold, where all the luggage was stored, Kasya let Sophie, Grace and Quintus out.

"Where are we?" whispered Grace.

"On board. But you can't stay here," Kasya replied. "You have to come below to the bilge. Sorry. It's not designed for humans to live in at all."

"What's a bilge?"

"It's the lowest of the low places in the boat," said Quintus. "All the dirt and rubbish gathers there. And the rats. The camel market smelt like a flower bed compared to this."

He was right. Even with her fingers clamped to her nose, Grace found that breathing through her mouth made her feel sick. At least Grace could console herself that she was heading in the same direction and in the same boat as Eleanor and Harry. She could make a pretence of being free, whereas she knew the others were prisoners. And Sophie kept most of the rats away.

There was something else that comforted Grace as well, that she didn't quite understand. It felt like the Phoenix was talking to her again. No, not talking, but present. A comfort.

The Phoenix - the Golden Phoenix not the White Phoenix from their own time - was following the boat across the Mediterranean. Kasya saw it high in the sky. Sometimes it would swoop down towards the mast of the boat. Then it would hover above the galley slaves at the oars, permanently chained in unbearable servitude. Kasya had the privilege of travelling in Cleopatra's state rooms (even though she and her mother slept on the floor) and she witnessed the drama with the bird on the second day. And in the bilge, Grace felt the fear of the Phoenix.

Neos had travelled in luxury with his mother and had watched the Phoenix following the boat day after day. The beautiful golden creature gave him an uneasy feeling. He wanted to be rid of it. Eventually he hit on a plan - a plan he liked the more he thought about it.

Most of the ship's passengers watched the Phoenix flying, including Caesar's and Cleopatra's personal guards. Neos began to talk to two of Caesar's archers.

"I bet you couldn't shoot that bird," he said to them.

"Easy enough," boasted the first.

"I agree," said the other, "but ain't it a special Egyptian bird? I've seen some of the Egyptian crew look at it like they was worshipping it."

"Maybe," said Neos. "That doesn't stop Caesar wanting it to go away. It's annoying him and he wants it dead," he lied. "And

Caesar's wishes should be anticipated, shouldn't they?"

"They should," agreed the first archer. "And why not have some fun at the same time!"

"Then this goes to the first of you to hit the bird," said Neos, showing them a gold coin with the face of Caesar on it. "I'll flip it to see who goes first."

Other soldiers and sailors on board gathered round and started to bet on the outcome.

Kasya saw the first archer take aim at the Phoenix as it circled above the mast. Was it possible this magnificent and unique bird would be killed by a lowly archer? She looked round desperately for someone to help, and saw Nicomachus standing in his usual place at the stern.

As she ran she saw the archer loose his arrow. It brushed through the Phoenix's tail feathers, causing golden sparks to fly.

"Look at that!" said the archer. "Maybe it really is a sacred bird. Maybe we'd better stop."

"Nah!" said the second archer. "You 'eard what the boy said. Caesar wants it dead. Get out of the way, it's my turn now."

Kasya pushed through the crowd and ran straight to Nicomachus.

"They're going to shoot the Phoenix!" she gasped.

Nicomachus moved swiftly. He pushed his way back through the crowd surrounding the archers, who were all cheering now. The second archer was taking aim, kneeling on the deck. Nicomachus kicked him in the back just as the arrow was unleashed. The bow swung wildly and the arrow splashed harmlessly into the sea. A great laugh went up from the crowd.

"Ho! Didn't see that coming, did you?" grinned the first archer.

"I'll have the hide off you, old man," growled the second

archer, rubbing his back. "What you do that for?"

"Don't you know this is the Phoenix?" shouted Nicomachus. "The Phoenix is sacred! Even shooting at this bird will have angered the gods! Had you killed it you would have suffered eternal damnation in this life and the next."

Nicomachus's words alone were enough to scare the archer, but as they were spoken the colour drained from his face and the crowd fell silent. The incident had caught Caesar's attention. The men around the archers parted like leaves in the wind as he walked toward them.

Caesar looked down on the two archers. His voice was icy cold. "Well, you will certainly have damnation in this life. Armourer! Bring chains. Here we have two more galley slaves to join the others. This ship will be your home now forever, with none of the privileges of your rank again."

The archers fell on their knees. "But sir! We was told you wanted to be rid of the bird!" answered the first man.

"Another word," said Caesar, "and I will have your tongue torn from your mouth. Then you will lose your speech as well as your freedom."

Neos looked down from the galley's stern with a sly smile. A few words from him had condemned these two men. His words had made Caesar react. He had control over the man he hated. And Caesar had no idea. Sure, the Phoenix was still alive, but there was something more satisfying in this.

On the deck below, Kasya saw Neos's face, and wondered just what it was that had pleased him so much. Then her mother called her and Kasya turned away. She did not see the orange fire flare up in the boy's cat-like eyes.

26. Fear of Water

In the smelly darkness of the bilges, Grace had felt the Phoenix's sudden fear, and then its pity for the two archers so unjustly condemned. Of course she had no idea what had happened in the open air so far above her. All she knew was that the threat to the Phoenix had gone, and it was telling her "Have no fear. You are not alone." It comforted to Grace to think of the Phoenix flying in the sunlight. She put out her hand and touched Sophie. She was a comfort too.

"Grace," whispered Quintus beside her. "You need to know something. I've been worrying about it."

"What is it?" asked Grace.

"I can't swim."

"I can," answered Grace, not sure what the point of Quintus's blunt statement was.

"Good for you," said Quintus. "I've never learnt to swim."

"I could teach you," said Grace, trying to be helpful, but still not seeing the point.

"I'm not sure there'll be time," said Quintus. "I've been thinking about what Kasya said in the camel market, 'We'll dump you overboard and you will swim the last bit.'" Quintus mimicked Kasya's voice so accurately it made Grace giggle, but then she realised what Quintus was on about. She'd forgotten what Kasya had said. Although she had been wondering how they would get off the boat, she'd just assumed they would get back into the basket with Sophie.

"Do you really think we'll have to swim?"

Grace couldn't think of anything nicer than swimming in the Mediterranean sea after being in the bilges. It would be warm and they could wash all the dirt and the stink of the bilge away.

"I don't know, but we'd better practise here now. You need to get the movements right." Grace tried to remember when she had learnt to swim. "I think you'd better start with doggy paddle." Sophie whined. There was barely any light in the bilge, but they had become so accustomed to the dark that they could just about see each other's movements. "You'll need to hold your hands like this and do this motion." Grace began to move each arm up and down in imitation of the doggy paddle.

"But won't I sink?"

"Of course you won't. Your lungs will be full of air. You'll float."

"I will?"

"You will."

Quintus copied the movements Grace had been making. So did Sophie. She sat on her hind legs and haunches and started moving her front paws. They both saw the dog and laughed out loud.

"What are you doing?" a voice said fiercely.

Grace went cold with fear.

Thank goodness, it was Kasya. She said sternly, "Do you want to get caught?"

Quintus and Grace were so relieved that they giggled again. Kasya gave them a withering look, but it was too dark for them to see it. She'd brought some food with her, but she had a message as well.

"We're nearly at the harbour. Boats are gathering around the ship," she said.

"What sort of boats?" Grace asked.

"Boats selling things to the sailors," replied Kasya. "Fruit, wine, trinkets. Anything really. They're not meant to come to meet us but they always do. They're the first to bring news too," she added. "Rome is full of turmoil. There are all sorts of rumours, and they say that Caesar's going to declare himself King. They say it's his ambition to be crowned."

Quintus whistled. "That's unheard of!"

"But what's strange about that? Egypt has a Queen. And we have a Queen at home. Can't Rome have a King?" said Grace.

"Rome," said Quintus proudly, "is a Republic. We are free of the slavery of kings and emperors. "SPQR" is the symbol that leads our legions when they go to war. 'The Senate and People of Rome.' We do not have kings."

"Oh, like America then," said Grace, realising as she spoke that this would be meaningless to her friends. Fortunately they ignored her, saving the need to explain.

"Anyway," said Kasya. "It means loyalties are divided. Things are changing. One of the boats will take you on board after dark and then you'll have to find a way to discover where they're taking the rest of us. I'll come and get you, but I've got to go now."

Quintus asked, "Will I have to swim?" but it was too late. She had gone.

Kasya had left some food and they both tucked in and waited. Once they were fed, (there wasn't much and they were hungry), Grace realised why Caesar might be so keen on the Scroll. "The Scroll will make him all powerful. If Caesar's at war at home

149

and can control the creatures of The Nether World, nothing can stop him becoming King and controlling the whole world. No wonder he wants them."

"What?" said Quintus, his mouth half full of bread. "What are you talking about now?"

"Oh, of course, you don't know. Should I tell you, I wonder?"

"Tell me what?"

"I ought to consult the others first," said Grace, half-talking to herself.

"Well, I don't want to hear your stupid secret. Why would I want to?" snapped Quintus.

Grace realised that Quintus was upset at being excluded, and probably felt as frightened and lonely as she did. At least she had Sophie and the Phoenix. Quintus had no one. So far he'd just been a travelling companion. It was time he became part of the team.

"You've got to know about the Scroll sooner or later, so I'll tell you now," she said.

At least it kept his mind off the swimming.

27. Escape

At first Quintus didn't believe any of it, but bit by bit Grace explained. Quintus was astonished, awestruck, frightened, though he tried to cover it up with his usual cockiness.

"I've seen one of those Nether World creatures," he boasted. "In the harbour. A horrible serpent with three heads, devouring men."

"It must be the thing Harry was fighting!"

"In Rome, there are many gods, many temples," Quintus went on, "but I've never seen or heard anything like this before. Monsters from The Nether World! Caesar wanting to be King of Rome! And you say you don't belong to this time - you aren't even born yet? The world's turning upside down! How can we sort it out?"

Quintus seemed to have found new energy. He had a purpose again, a reason to be alive. For Grace, away from her cousins and her new friend Kasya, it was just a relief to share the problem. In the dark bilge, they shared other secrets and sorrows, the sadness and loneliness of being orphans.

"So what were your parents like?" asked Quintus.

Grace hesitated. "I try so hard to remember, but now they've been dead for nearly half my life. I'm terrified of forgetting them. I keep trying, but I can't be sure I'm actually remembering them. I imagine what I'd like them to be like now. I hope they'd like me." A lump came into her throat.

"Well, of course they would! They'd be proud of you!" said Quintus. He patted her shoulder awkwardly.

Grace hastily changed the subject. "What did your parents do, then?"

"My father was the best sewage engineer in Rome," said Quintus proudly. "That's why they asked him to go to Alexandria."

"Sewage? Poo?"

"Yes, poo," said Quintus. He said the word in a funny way, deliberately to make Grace laugh. "That's why Rome's the cleanest city in the Empire. We have the best sewers. And," Quintus leaned in whispering, "I know my way round all of them. I can move around Rome more quickly than anyone else. I'm never seen and never caught."

"In the sewers? Yuk!"

"They're no worse than in here! And you don't smell too good yourself!"

Footsteps close by silenced them. Fortunately, it was only Kasya. "We've got to go. Now."

"Pack your bags then, darling," Quintus replied, standing up in his clothes, the only possessions he had. As she picked up the bag she had been given in The Palace Library, Grace was glad he said that, otherwise she might have forgotten it.

"Come on! And be quiet!" Kasya said.

They climbed up some steep stairs lit by tiny lamps here and there. When they came out on deck they discovered it was night. The air was so refreshing that Grace breathed in deeply, only to regret it as the smell of body odour and unwashed men assaulted her nostrils. The children were standing on a platform in the middle of the banks of rowers. The men were swinging together in a steady beat to the sound of a drum. These galley slaves were permanently chained to their oars and paid them no attention.

The children crouched down under another set of stairs while Kasya checked the way was clear. Suddenly, they found themselves in the glamour of Cleopatra's state apartments. The air smelt of the Queen's musky perfume. Nicomachus was standing by an open window, where a rope was hanging down.

"Down you go," he whispered, giving them each a friendly pat. Quintus went first, then Grace and they tumbled into the boat below. Looking up, they saw Sophie with all four paws in a row on the cabin windowsill, nervously looking down at the drop. There was no way she could climb down a rope. She started to back away, but they saw Kasya give her a shove. Before Sophie knew what was happening she had fallen with legs spread-eagled on top of them. One of the boatmen threw a blanket over them and the boat moved away silently. They were free! But with each splash of the oars in the water, they were moving further and further away from Harry and Eleanor.

Once or twice, Quintus tried to talk to the men in the boat, but all the leader said was "Shut up!" They rowed through the rest of the night, then when the sun rose they saw they were off the coast.

"Out now!" The leading crewman pointed overboard.

"What about going to the shore?" cried Quintus. "I can't swim!"

"You'll learn quick enough. We've barely been paid enough to risk bringing you this far. This is as far as we go. Jump. Or we push you. Your choice."

"Here," said one of the rowers. "Could be you'll need food.

It's not much, but better than nothing." He tossed Quintus a parcel wrapped in a big green leaf.

"Thanks," said Quintus. "Here, Grace, you'd better take it. I'm going to need all my hands for swimming."

Sophie plunged eagerly into the water. Grace jumped after her, hoping her canvas bag and the package of food wouldn't be spoilt by the salt water. Once in the water, she turned, waiting for Quintus. She began to tread water, then she realised that she could touch the bottom. It was shallow all the way to the shore. Then she saw a boatman push Quintus into the water.

Quintus spluttered. His arms lashed out, making a huge noise in the water to no effect. Then he sank below the surface. Grace moved towards him, but he reappeared, with just enough breath to say "Help!" before disappearing below again. This time, Grace caught him and held his head above water. There was a big smile on her face. "How do you like your first swimming lesson?"

Quintus had already swallowed enough water to make him feel sick. "You go on," he gasped dramatically, "Leave me. I'll never make it."

"OK," grinned Grace, dropping his head just enough for it to fall under water a little bit.

"Noooo!"

"Can you walk?"

"Of course, I can walk," dribbled Quintus, as Grace held his head again. "I just can't swim."

"Then walk," said Grace, dropping him. Quintus sank again, with more splashes and spluttering. This time she pulled him up by his hair. Then suddenly he found his feet. He breathed in deeply. "I'm going to get you for that!"

Grace knew that it was much quicker to swim than walk when chest-high in water, so there was no chance that Quintus

154

was going to catch her. She swam to the shore and then spent some time watching him wade in, all the while laughing and throwing pebbles at him, not hitting him all the time.

As Quintus emerged from the water, he shouted something. Grace prepared to make a dash for it, knowing that Quintus would want to pay her back, but then she saw that something was wrong. Quintus's mouth was wide open and he was pointing behind her. Grace turned.

The land was black and brown and moving, a shadow of black flowing down to the sea. Birds. Hundreds and thousands of starlings were all around, gathering further and further up the hills behind her. Grace froze as Quintus came up to her. The birds gathered round them, leaving a small semicircle of sand between the children and the sea. They were still. They didn't chirp. They didn't move away. They just stared, their tiny bright eyes blinking occasionally.

Grace took a step forward. Nothing happened. Then another. Nothing. Grace ran towards the birds. They should have flown away, but they just parted silently, barely moving, leaving a path.

"Come on," said Grace. "They're going to get out of the way! Which way do we go?"

Quintus looked at the sun, then pointed. "That way, I think."

Grace went forward, Quintus following. As they passed, the birds moved so that there was always a circle of grass clear around them to walk on. "Is this the right way?" asked Grace. Quintus nodded.

After a while they ran into trouble. "We're veering away from the road. The birds are making us go up the hill," said Quintus.

"Well let's try to move back on the right track," answered Grace. They tried to walk back down the hill. Each time they did, the birds rose up like a wall, blocking them, unwavering.

"What shall we do?" whispered Grace. They stepped back and the wall of birds dropped away. The circle of grass around them changed shape and pushed them on a predefined path. The birds followed close behind, but grass showed through ahead of the children. Quintus walked on a little and the path ahead opened up even more. "They're telling us where to go. See?"

"But it's not the way we want to go, is it?" answered Grace.

"Let's think positively," said Quintus bravely. "Maybe the birds are on our side and are showing us where to go."

"Maybe they're not, and they're taking us into danger. How do we know?"

As Grace spoke, several birds rose up behind them and prodded them, a whole series of gentle nudges down their backs.

"Well," said Quintus. "I don't think we have a choice." They marched on up the hill and the prodding stopped. "I think if they weren't on our side they could be a lot more frightening too. Just look at the numbers of birds swooping down over there." He pointed ahead. They could see a long ribbon of road winding between the hills. "That must be the road to Rome."

Before long, the starlings had brought the two of them to a point high above the road, near some boulders. The children were forced to stop and a group of birds surrounded them whilst more and more moved away towards the road.

"Oh!" said Grace suddenly.

"What?"

"It's the Phoenix!" Grace looked up. Sure enough, high in the sky above the birds, was a tiny golden shape.

"It's all right," she said, thankfully. "He's telling me to trust the birds. He says we're not alone."

"Look! It's Cleopatra's household on the road," said Quintus, "but I can't see Caesar or his guards anywhere." Grace tried to identify people on the crowded road. She thought she could see Harry and Eleanor with Hypatia and Nicomachus and some heavily armed guards. Neos was there too, slightly apart from the others, as she might have expected.

Harry and Eleanor were in the column. They were tired and hungry from the long march from the harbour. They were still prisoners and although Harry's burns were beginning to heal, they were sore. Prisoners or not, both the children became aware that all was not well with the reception Caesar had received at the harbour. Kasya had managed to tell them a little of what was going on from the gossip she had overheard.

Caesar had his own guard, of course, but they had been greeted at the harbour by a heavily armed deputation from the Senate, asking for Caesar to report to them immediately about the rumours that he was going to declare himself King.

"If they could have, they'd have arrested him then and there, I think," Kasya said, "but they couldn't do that with his own men looking after him. Caesar took command of the situation, though. He said he was going to march to Rome and interview the Senate himself."

"That's why he's so great," Harry said. "He just takes over and turns everything to his advantage." He couldn't help admiring Caesar, even though he knew how ruthless he could be.

"Anyway, he's gone," said Kasya.

Like everyone else in the column, Harry and Grace had noticed the birds along the roadside, silently landing all along the sides of the column and covering the hillsides like a slick of shimmering oil. The normally noisy household was ill at ease.

Suddenly the black slick on the hillside came alive and threw itself up into the air in a dramatic murmuration. The birds swooped as one before forming a huge pattern that created a tunnel - a tunnel without an entry or an exit around the column. The birds pressed closer and closer to the people in the column, blotting out the sunlight. People were trying to swat them away like mosquitoes. Even the guards broke ranks, nearly driven mad by the drone of wings and the nearness of the starlings that drove out light and even air. All except Nicomachus, Harry and Eleanor. The birds guided them and bunched them together. Nicomachus tried to hold on to Hypatia and Kasya to bring them too, but the birds were too strong, too determined. Hypatia and Kasya were left behind.

Eleanor was first to realise that the birds around the three of them were making a pathway up the hill. The 'tunnel' above them thinned enough to spread some light on the ground and the little group was gently pressed by the birds into moving away from the column up into the hills where Grace and Quintus were hiding.

The birds guided Harry, Eleanor and Nicomachus into a cave behind the boulders. As they stooped to enter, Quintus said, "Get back, Grace! We don't know if they're friend or foe!"

But Grace had already recognised her cousins and the tall figure with them

"Oh, Eleanor! Harry! Is it really you? And Nicomachus!" She was almost crying with joy and relief. She and Eleanor hugged each other tightly.

Harry was looking at Quintus. "Who are you?"

Quintus stared back defiantly.

"Oh, Harry, this is Quintus," said Grace He's a friend of Kasya's. His father was a - "

"My father was the best engineer in Rome," boasted Quintus.

"He taught me to find my way around the city without ever going into the streets."

"How - " began Harry, but Grace cut him short. "Quintus's dad was a sewerage engineer. Kasya brought Quintus with Sophie and me. She thinks he'll be useful in Rome. And by the way, I've told him about the Scroll and everything."

"You did what?" demanded Harry, but Nicomachus laid a hand on his shoulder.

"If you're a friend of Kasya's, that's good enough for me," the old man said. "And your knowledge of Rome will be useful. I'm sure I don't need to tell you how to keep secrets."

"No, sir," Quintus said politely.

Suddenly the light disappeared and the cave was pitch dark. The entrance was blocked by the wall of birds.

"How are we going to get out of this cave?" demanded Harry. "The birds have us trapped."

It was true. They might have escaped from Cleopatra's guards but they were prisoners in the dark.

Then Eleanor screamed.

28. Underground

"There's something in my hair! Get it out! Get it out!" shrieked Eleanor.

Nicomachus was closest and ran his hands over her head and face. Something flapped away. "It's gone," he said, but in the darkness Eleanor was still gasping.

"It's probably bats," whispered Quintus. "There are lots of bats in caves."

"Like that's a comfort," said Eleanor shakily. "I wish we could get out."

Once or twice, one of them had returned to the front of the cave to try and escape, but every time the birds pushed them back, gently but firmly. The birds kept the wall intact. The movement of their wings let in air, but no light. This was not just any darkness, but an inky, thorough, complete darkness. There was no difference between opening your eyes and shutting your eyes. Just darkness. Grace had opened the leafy parcel of food and found some bread, cheese and a coarse sort of sausage inside. They had shared it round, but no one ate much because there was nothing to drink and they were beginning to be thirsty.

"Can you see anything, Nicomachus?" asked Eleanor, calmer now.

"Of course he can't see anything," said Quintus scornfully.

The others were silent, but Nicomachus knew what Eleanor meant. Could he use his foresight to see into the future, to know what the future held for them?

"Maybe if there were some light, I could use the mirror," he answered Eleanor, "but I can see nothing. Yet it's not just nothing. I don't feel fear, though. I think we're being hidden, not trapped. And yet, I also feel the world is changing. Something is happening which is out of our control. A great evil is ending but another is beginning."

"Thanks," said Quintus sarcastically, "That's really cheered me up."

All at once the birds outside the cave separated like a curtain. Welcome light streamed in, but only for a moment. It was soon pitch black again. Then there were wings flapping, different wings.

"There's something else here with us," said Harry, trying to keep his voice steady. He was as afraid as Eleanor, but determined to be brave.

"What is it? If it comes near me, I'll scream," said Eleanor.

Then Grace let out a breath. "It's OK."

"Well, that's reassuring." Quintus's voice was slightly too high-pitched to be normal.

"Yes, it's the Phoenix. He's here. He's come back. He organised all those other birds to protect us. And he doesn't want us to go out. We need to go further in. Come on."

Grace led the way. In fact, the Phoenix led the way, flying in front of them just far enough ahead so they could hear his wings flapping slowly. They all stumbled and fell over rocks and boulders in the darkness, stubbing toes, grazing knees and elbows. Slowly the path, which ran downhill all the way, grew clearer. The noise of their feet echoed on a path paved with smooth stone. They turned a corner and entered a large and beautiful chamber. There was just enough light to see again. Where the light in came from wasn't obvious, but a faint green glow emanated from the walls, similar to the light in Alexander's tomb.

Quintus whistled, and began to walk around. His hands touched the cold smooth stone of tall pillars supporting a vaulted ceiling, but as he looked up, he saw that the roof - the whole room - was carved entirely out of stone.

"It's just like one of the city's storm drains," he muttered.

"Is it?" asked Harry.

"Is it what?" asked Quintus, unaware he had spoken out loud.

"A storm drain."

"Well it looks exactly like one. I've explored them often enough in Rome. But this isn't one."

"How can you tell?"

"It's in the wrong place. We're above Rome in these hills, too high up for a storm drain. They were built below the city to carry the water away when it rains. This room is bone dry." Quintus bent down and put his hand on the stone floor. The other children copied him. It was cold, but quite dry. "See."

"So what is it?"

Quintus didn't answer immediately, but went on looking around. "Look. I know the sewers, drains and tunnels around Rome as well as anyone. My father worked them, and so did my grandfather. They've been my playground all my life. This cavern is something different. It doesn't belong here. It's like it's a secret."

Eleanor had been going around the edge of the room, running

162

her hands along the walls. It was smooth like masonry, but suddenly her hands felt something different, strange markings. She stopped to feel them more closely, tracing the indents.

A hand grasped Eleanor's fingers. She froze in fear, but the hand, gnarled and dirty, traced her forefinger over the next symbol. "It's mine, that one," a voice said. Eleanor screamed. The owner of the hand sprang back and fell to the floor. As the others reached him, Harry stamped his foot on the man's arm to stop him getting up. It was a ragged, pathetic old man in filthy clothes.

"Are you going to kill me like the others? Please don't kill me," he begged.

"Of course we're not going to kill you! Of course not." But Harry didn't take his foot off the old man's arm, not yet.

Quintus was by the wall looking at the strange markings. He ran his own fingers across them. "Seven of them! It can't be! These men vanished years ago. Years before I was born. The rumours were true."

"What rumours? What men? What do you mean?"

"When I was little, my father told me a story about seven stonemasons who worked on the sewers and drains when he was first an apprentice, maybe thirty or forty years ago. They were the best men working at the time. One day they were specially selected and called away for a job. Then they just vanished. They were never seen again. It was said that one of them reappeared in Rome with tales of the secret cavern they had built. And stories about all the masons being murdered except him. No one believed him and then he vanished and it was forgotten."

"So what have these marks to do with them?"

"These are the marks of the seven stonemasons who vanished. They must have built this chamber. So the stories were true.

But why?"

A frail voice spoke from the floor. "Yes, the rumours were true, but no one believed me when I escaped. Then all my family were murdered. Then the man who commissioned this room died, drowned in one of the city drains. He was a senator who built this room as a secret hiding place. His death will be on my conscience, but it troubles me little, as he killed my family to hide a secret. Now the room is mine. It has been mine alone since then - until now."

The old man's voice echoed in a peculiar way. He spoke into the floor and it reverberated all around the room. Harry released his arm. The voice was clearer now, but the man looked and smelt like a tramp. "Do you like my home? I have been alone here for too long and I'm afraid to go out in daylight in case they find me. I had thought I was the only one to know about this place, but now you are here. Please don't kill me!" He crouched down, his arms over his head in terror as Harry stood above him.

"We're not going to harm you. Really." said Harry, squatting down next to him.

The man turned his head toward Harry. Now it was Harry's turn to be afraid. The old man's eyes were cloudy white, the colour of milk, with no iris or pupil at all. The man couldn't see his fear. Instead he put out his hand to fumble and grope, finding Harry's arm and holding him. "Do you have any food?"

"You're blind?" asked Harry.

"Yes, I'm blind, but it doesn't make any difference. I don't need sight in these caves and catacombs. But I do need food. The winter has been harsh this year for gathering scraps." His thin old voice took on a pleading note. "Please - give me food and keep me company. My house will be your house."

There was still a bit of bread and sausage left. "It's not very nice, but do take it." Grace put the bread into his hands. To her surprise he only nibbled it.

"I thought you said you were hungry?"

"I am," he mumbled through his mouthful, "but I never eat it all. There might not be any more, you see."

"Tell me," said Nicomachus, "has anyone ever found you here? Do people come here?"

"No, no, never," the old man replied hastily.

Nicomachus took his hand and commanded, "Look at me." The white eyes looked up towards Nicomachus's voice as the librarian and last priest of his sect looked into him, beyond the eyes, into his mind.

"He speaks the truth," said Nicomachus. "Maybe our luck has changed. This can be our home and our base while we work out how to recover the Scroll and prevent the damage from it being in the very worst of hands. Here, we can make our plans for the future."

29. The Babel Charms

They had moved to the back to the cavern, preferring to be within reach of outside. The birds had gone and Sophie was guarding the entrance. She lay down outside, regularly sniffing the air, ready to bark if anyone approached. The four children, Harry, Eleanor, Grace and Quintus sat in a small circle. Nicomachus was tending to the old man, trying to find out more from him. He was occasionally sensible and lucid, more often distant. He treated the last portion of bread Grace had given him like a comfort blanket, sucking on it rather than eating it.

"Here's the bag I brought from The Palace Library," said Grace, pulling it towards her and peering into it like a Christmas stocking. "It's got our things in it from before, from the last time."

She pulled out the dagger first, the one that had been given to Eleanor the previous year by Edgar the Librarian. The dagger had been made for Eleanor of Aquitaine, Queen of England by Edwin the Blacksmith, a man who had become the children's friend. It was in its own sheath, hanging from a leather belt. Eleanor buckled the belt around her waist and drew the short blade from its scabbard. All three children looked at it. The blade was a bright shining silver-grey. Harry, Eleanor and Grace gave each other knowing looks, relieved.

"Can I see it?" asked Quintus, holding his hand out.

"Sure," said Eleanor, passing it to him. "The blade was made …" She hesitated. Should she say 'will be made?' That would confuse everyone, including herself. She went on, "The blade was made from a shard of a famous sword called Ascalon. It glows green in the presence of treachery and traitors."

"It's not glowing green now," said Quintus, turning it over in his hands. Then he scowled at the three children from the future. "That's why you were looking at it so carefully! You want to know if you can trust us."

"We didn't mean to be rude," said Grace, hurriedly. "It's just that - "

"Don't worry," said Quintus, feeling better after her apology. "It's sensible. And it means the old man can be trusted too doesn't it?" He handed the weapon back to Eleanor.

"And Nicomachus," said Eleanor, slipping the dagger back into its sheath. "We really know we're a team now. As if we didn't anyway, after all that's happened. I just hope Kasya and Hypatia are safe. There certainly wasn't the welcome that Caesar hoped for at the port. He was quite angry that Cleopatra wasn't given the reception he wanted."

Then Grace pulled out the chain mail that Edwin the blacksmith had given Harry. Harry's fingers ran over the individual links in the armour, feeling it gently. It was so light and flexible, it felt more like fabric than armour. He slipped the silvery metal over his head like a jumper. It looked strange over his grubby Egyptian clothes, but as he moved around, he was reminded just how light it was. Quintus put his hand out to touch it, then pulled back nervously before saying, "Can I?"

"Go ahead," said Harry.

Quintus fingered the cold metal. "It's nothing like our

Roman armour. Where did you get it?"

"That's another story," said Harry, turning Quintus's attention away from him by saying, "And your gift from the Library, Grace. Have you got that?"

Grace patted her chest where the golden clock and compass hung. She could feel it next to the tiny translation necklace, still hidden under her shirt.

"There's one more thing in the bag too. It's for Harry." She took the small brown paper parcel from the bag. It was the one that had been on Great Uncle Jasper's desk in the big house before they embarked on this adventure. Harry turned it over in his hands before undoing the tight knot with his teeth and then tearing off the paper. A plain box was within it. Inside was an object Harry instantly recognised, now with a silver mount and a long chain attached. He pulled it out.

"Yuk!" said Grace, looking at the object. "That looks like an old finger's been mounted as a necklace. What was Great Uncle Jasper thinking!"

"It's not a finger, Grace."

"Well, it looks like one."

"Ah," said Eleanor. "I know what it is. It's the dragon's toe and claw. The one that scratched your arm and poisoned you last year. It is a bit gruesome. Rather odd of Great Uncle Jasper to put it on a necklace."

Quintus's eyes opened wide. "An actual dragon? Really? I thought they were just in stories."

"Yes," said Harry, suddenly feeling shy. He hastily put the chain over his neck, tucking the trophy under his chain mail. "I guess he thought it might come in useful, so I might as well look after it."

Nicomachus had left the old man to sleep and now stood at

the edge of their circle.

"May I see?" he asked.

Harry drew the chain out from under his shirt. As he did so, his translation necklace became tangled with the chain, so he pulled both over his head and began to untangle the two, pulling at the knotted chains.

To Harry's surprise, Nicomachus reached out and grabbed the necklaces, snatching them from Harry's hand.

"Oi!" shouted Harry, rubbing his hand. "Why did you do that?"

Nicomachus was looking at the necklaces. "Where did you get this?" he shouted, uncharacteristically angry.

Harry shook his head. "He's got my necklace. I can't understand what he's saying."

"He's asking you where you got them," said Eleanor.

"Well, ask him to give them back and then I can tell him!"

"They're his - both of them," Eleanor said to Nicomachus. "He won one. The other - " Eleanor tried to work out how to explain. "The other came from The Palace Library. At least, I suppose it must have."

"But that's impossible!" said Nicomachus, more to himself than to Harry. "This necklace is almost unique. Only three were ever made. This is one of the Babel Charms, the key to reading Alexander's Scroll, the only way to unlock the secrets." Still holding Harry's necklaces, he fumbled in the satchel he had kept with him all the time. He took out the tiny ivory box that Eleanor had seen him put in the satchel when they were together in his study. He fiddled with a hidden lock and opened it. It was empty.

Nicomachus stared. "They are gone! This is impossible! There were only three. The most closely guarded secret! No one alive knows about these! How can this box be empty? All three were there and it has never left my side." He looked up at Harry, now more confused than angry. "Eleanor. You could read the Scroll? Both of you?"

"Yes," said Eleanor, nervous and confused. "Yes, we could."

"So," said Nicomachus, "Do you have a necklace like this?" His voice sounded more kindly now, more gently spoken, but with a fierce intensity.

"Yes," replied Eleanor.

Harry said, "They were given to us, magically, I suppose. We didn't steal them."

"Eleanor," said Nicomachus again, working things through in his mind. "You said you came from the future?" Eleanor nodded. "Then these necklaces, which contain the Babel Charms, are the same necklaces. If you have them in the future they cannot exist in two places at once - not for long at least. Once you had brought them here, our necklaces from the past, the necklaces that Alexander and I found on our travels could not exist in the same time. But tell me, Grace - please reassure me. Do you have one too?"

Grace drew her necklace from underneath her own shirt.

Nicomachus let out a breath. "That is a relief. They are all accounted for."

Quintus looked from Nicomachus to the children. "Could one of you explain to me just what is going on here? I'm only a poor Roman sewer rat. Magic charms, let alone time travel, are a bit out of my league."

They laughed at that and the tension cleared. Nicomachus handed back Harry's necklaces.

"That's better," said Harry, smiling rather ruefully. "I hated not being able to understand you."

"I know," said Nicomachus. "I am sorry. But it was a shock, you understand. I think it's time I told you more. I cannot explain the time travel, nor the mysteries of deep magic or the workings of the gods, but I think it is time to share more of my story with you. It follows on from what I told Eleanor, that I know she shared with you.

"After we had discovered the Scroll which Neos has now taken, Alexander and his armies swept back towards the West and into Babylonia. There we were to find the key to reading that Scroll at a place known to the Babylonians as the Temple of the Seven Lights of Earth. There was a great ziggurat, a huge tower, half-ruined, It dwarfed the lighthouse at Pharos in Alexandria. The Hebrews called it the Tower of Babel. Their stories told that all men once spoke a common language and shared their knowledge and power. They became so arrogant that they planned to build a tower that would reach to Heaven and challenge God Himself. Their God stopped the tower being built and, to confuse them and prevent them from committing this sacrilege, He gave them all different languages so that they could not understand one another.

"Perhaps we had become too arrogant as well, for Alexander gave the order for the Tower to be rebuilt. But then he died and the project was never completed. However, there was a caste of priests who lived in the ruins of Babel. They shared a secret with me. They told us that they were the guardians of the One Language; that they knew the way for all men to communicate. Alexander had become close to these priests and they accompanied his body back to Alexandria, bringing their secrets with them - especially the tiny pieces of papyrus within your necklaces that hold the magic of universal language.

"These same priests were the ones I joined at the foundation of the Library of Alexandria. The Babel Charms were our secret to translating books from around the known world. Only a few of us knew of the existence of the Charms, and we swore never to reveal that we had them. You are the only living people with whom I have ever shared this knowledge. Since the Charms have found their way to you, you should know their magical power.

"Wearing them is the only way to read Alexander's Scroll. These Charms are what Caesar and Cleopatra need. Neos will be looking for them too, although none of them know exactly what it is they are looking for. Only with these Charms can they read the Scroll to unleash the evil powers of The Nether World fully. Only with these Charms can they discover how to defeat the monsters of that world. That is why Alexander's Scroll must be protected and only as a last resort should it and the Babel Charms be destroyed. We must return Alexander's Scroll to trusted hands, out of the way of those seeking power."

"But, Nicomachus," said Harry "wouldn't it just be easier to destroy it all? Then no one can ever use them for evil again?"

"I've often thought that," said Nicomachus, "but it's not possible to see far into the future and what might be needed at some distant time. Why was the magic of Alexander's Scroll written down in the past? Because its secrets were needed. Who would know how to destroy that evil, like the savage cat of Cleopatra's which has found its way into her soul as well as Neos's. The good often need the same tools as the bad."

"So, we need to make a plan to get the Scroll back," said Harry.

"Yes. Whatever we decide, it will be dangerous."

30. Confessions

"There is more you need to know," added Nicomachus. He sighed, as if exhausted by what he was telling them. "Then my confessions will be complete.

"When the Library of Alexandria was first opened there were three groups of people who shared the knowledge of Alexander's Scroll and the Babel Charms. I was among a few of the Greeks schooled in the arts of war and of philosophy. We brought our knowledge from Greece to the Library. And of course we brought Alexander's Scroll from the East, hidden in his tomb. Then there were the priests from Babylonia, who had looked after and grown close to Alexander in his final year. They were the guardians of the Babel Charms and the knowledge of language.

"Together, we founded the Library of Alexandria, the greatest library in the world until it was so callously burnt down. We were also founders of the Cult of Serapis, in which Greek and Egyptian gods were merged, which gave our library a sense of holy purpose and mysticism. And so the Temple of Serapis and the Library of Alexandria became one.

"But there was another group of people who became important to the culture of the Library. When Ptolemy I, Cleopatra's ancestor, had installed himself as Pharaoh, priests from the most ancient parts of Egypt came to Alexandria looking for more information about him; and reassurance also. They found little to trust, but they came with another secret, a more profound secret, uncovered by their predecessors thousands of years before. We installed them in their own quarters in the Library and over many years trust grew between us all. The priests were growing old - all except one, who remained graceful and ageless. Though he appeared to be the youngest, he was their leader. They looked up to him.

"Eventually, they trusted us enough. It was the young-looking priest who came to see me. He offered to create a new brotherhood, but it would require the most sacred oaths before their knowledge could be shared. We agreed, and so these three groups became one. I am the last of that brotherhood, the last of those guardians, so once again I need to share my burdens. I have told you about two of the secrets. There is a third, but first it is time for a new brotherhood."

"With sisters," interrupted Eleanor.

"With sisters, Eleanor. OK?" said Nicomachus, smiling.

Eleanor giggled. "OK!"

"But it can't be a sisterhood either," said Quintus.

"Then we shall have new guardians," said Grace simply, "Guardians of the Scroll." It was said in a sudden moment of inspiration, but as Grace said the words, she thought back to the things she had heard on her own in The Palace Library when Harry and Eleanor had disappeared. There they had talked about the Council of the Book. It crossed Grace's mind that maybe they were one and the same in different times, for who talked about scrolls in modern England? For now, however, she decided to keep that thought to herself.

"But how do you know you can trust us?" asked Harry

seriously. "You hardly know us."

"The simple fact that you ask the question is good confirmation that I should be able to trust you. Kasya and Hypatia I know well. We will need to trust them and also find them and free them. I trust their judgement too - which brings Quintus into this group. But more than that, my foresight tells me to trust you. Now, are you prepared to take the oaths?"

They sat in a solemn circle and Nicomachus put his hands out to each side, palms up. Instinctively, Harry took his own hand and put it into Nicomachus's. He held his other hand out in the same way and suddenly all of them understood and all sat with hands joined.

"Now," said Nicomachus. "We will form the Guardians. We promise to each other that we will protect each other, but above all, we will protect the secrets of the Scroll from evil throughout time."

Once he had said the words, he asked each of the others to speak them in turn.

"Now swear by the gods you hold most sacred that you will keep your promise. I swear by the great god Serapis and Alexander Ammon that I will keep faith."

The three children looked at each other. "I swear in the name of Our Lord that I will keep faith," said Harry, and Eleanor and Grace repeated his words.

"I swear by Rome's Twelve Gods that I will keep faith," said Quintus.

"Well done. Now we are brothers - and sisters," said Nicomachus. "Now I may tell you the last secret.

"The priests of the ancient pharaohs had a secret that some might consider greater even than Alexander's Scroll. They had unlocked the secret of immortality. Immortality, the ambition of the powerful, and the curse of the unwary or unwise."

"Unwise like you?" asked Eleanor, "Unwise because all around you die while you survive?" Then she blushed. "I'm sorry -I didn't mean to sound cheeky, Nicomachus!"

Nicomachus replied, "You are not cheeky, Eleanor. It was a good question. Perhaps I was unwise, but the 'young' priest of the Pharaohs was living proof of the secret of immortality. Someone else was needed to carry on the secret, however, for it turns out that the potion - for that it what it is - does not actually grant immortality, just extreme longevity. I am over four hundred years old. He was more than a thousand years when he died some two hundred years ago. And by then, as you can imagine, I was lonely."

Quintus whistled. "A thousand years! Imagine living that long!"

"Thousands of years before, the Pharaohs had continually sought immortality. These ancient priests were a group trained to search for the secrets of eternal life. They explored this for generations, as they watched Pharaohs rule over their people. The priests saw that the longer the Pharaoh ruled, the more autocratic and even evil his reign became. The priests decided that, if they ever discovered it, immortality was a secret that should be guarded. For generations, it did not matter, there was no way of achieving it. Instead of immortality in this world, they offered immortality in the afterlife - the art of embalming bodies so that the Pharaohs would be preserved as mummies. The priests became more and more skilled at this and the Pharaohs built larger and larger tombs to house their mummies, preserved forever, permanent as the Pyramids at Giza. This itself became an obsession. But then, some of the priests actually created - and successfully tested - the potion of immortality.

It took many years, of course, to see how some of them aged - or did not - but during that time, they realised the dangers of sharing the potion with the Pharaohs. Instead they founded a brotherhood to keep the secret.

"Some of them wanted to destroy everything, feeling that immortality was disrespectful to the gods. In the end it was agreed that the recipe for the potion would be destroyed, but that two vials of it would be kept and preserved secretly."

"So where are the vials now?" asked Harry.

"That is the problem," sighed Nicomachus. "The two vials are hidden in the two ends of the Alexander Scroll."

"So Neos has the potion too?"

"Yes," sighed Nicomachus. "But on the other hand he cannot use it, if he does not know it is there. If he does find it, he is unlikely to taste it."

"Why not?"

"The potion was purposely made with a disgusting smell and taste - like a poison. It is a final safeguard to protect the potion - and to make the unwary and the unwise think again."

Harry had a weary sense of déjà-vu in being set an impossible task once more. "We have to steal the Scroll from Neos, who'll be at Caesar and Cleopatra's villa, the most closely guarded place in Rome, which houses the two most powerful people in the world. We don't even know where the villa is. And we have to face up to that foul cat too."

"There is a way to destroy the cat," said Nicomachus. "It is a creature of The Nether World and the secret to controlling such animals is in the Alexander Scroll."

"Which we have not got!" interrupted Eleanor impatiently. "And you said the cat was immortal."

"Indeed. But I have read the Scroll - all of it, and it is clear in

177

my mind. We know that to control the cat, you must defeat it in battle, as Ptolemy did, but to kill it, something else is needed."

"But how can you kill it if it's an immortal animal?" asked Harry.

"It's immortal, not invincible!" replied Nicomachus. "But like many creatures of The Nether World, only a special weapon or tool will destroy them. Until just a few moments ago I never dreamt we could have such a tool, but I now believe we have one. Harry, pass me your necklace again for a moment if you please."

Harry handed the necklace back to Nicomachus who looked at the gruesome claw in detail. "And this is really a dragon's claw?" Harry nodded. "You see," Nicomachus continued, "only the venom of a dragon can kill the immortal cat. In this claw, underneath the sharp nail, is the venom of a dragon. There is another ingredient too." Nicomachus paused, not for dramatic effect, but because so much talking tired him. "The venom must be delivered by a dragon-slayer."

Harry's face fell, but not before Eleanor spoke up excitedly, "Well, Harry's a dragon slayer!"

"Not really," muttered Harry weakly.

Then another voice broke in, a voice they had forgotten about.

31. Reconnaissance

"I hope I'm not disturbing you, but I was just listening to what you were saying. Would it help if I told you there's a tunnel from this room to the Villa Appia?" The old blind mason continued without waiting for a reply, "Sorry. I think I was a bit mad just now. It's amazing how a little bit of food can make you feel more normal again. I haven't had any bread for years. Just rats. Sometimes fat rats, mind you, but you never can be sure where they've been. Well actually, you can be sure. They've come up from the sewers, but I don't really like to think about it too much."

The children thought he sounded nearly as mad as he had before. Why suddenly start talking about this Villa Appia?

It was Quintus who questioned it first. "Caesar's Villa? The big one on the Appian Way just outside the walls of the city?"

"That's the one," said the mason, proudly.

"That's where Cleopatra's stayed before. The last time she was in Rome. She hosted hundreds of parties. She was the talk of the town, admired and reviled about equally by the top of Roman society," said Quintus, "but I bet the ones who reviled her weren't invited to her parties. I bet that's where she's staying again."

"I thought you might be interested when I heard you talking

about Cleopatra," said the mason. "The tunnel goes right up to the Villa's kitchens. There's a secret door there. You can hear the slaves talking sometimes if they're shouting a bit. I've often thought of creeping in and pinching a bit of food, but - " He stopped.

"But?" asked Quintus.

The old man hung his head. "Well I've never been brave enough. The tunnel's never been used since it was built. If I'd opened the door, they would have killed me. The thing is, I've always felt safe down here, ever since they took away all my friends. No one's ever discovered the door from the other side."

"So how do you know it's a door?" asked Harry.

"I built it," the old man said proudly. "One of my finest pieces of work. It's a heavy door that swings so easily on a central spindle even a child push it open. But only if you know how."

"Good. So you'll be able to show us?" asked Harry.

The old man looked terrified, so much so that they thought he might go completely mad again. "Oh no. No. No. NO! I can't do that! I have to hide."

Eleanor went over to him and calmed him down. "I'm sure we'll only ask you if it's absolutely necessary," she said.

"It will be," said Harry, under his breath. He looked around the group, the new Guardians and this old man, who had heard everything they said. Nicomachus looked exhausted after his confessions and the journey. They were all thirsty and they simply didn't have enough information about what was going on, let alone any idea about how they were going to win back the Alexander Scroll from Neos. Or would it now be in the hands of Cleopatra? Someone had to take charge.

"We need to know more and we need food," he said firmly. "Let's work in pairs. Eleanor and Grace, take Sophie just as soon

180

as it's dusk and go and hunt for some rabbits or something. Anything for us to eat in here. I don't fancy eating rats. And water. Quintus, you and I will use your contacts in Rome to find out what's happening from anyone you know. From the way the mason talked about feeding on rats, there must be another exit from this place to the sewers. Is that right?" Harry looked across at the old mason, who nodded and pointed to the far end of the chamber. "Good. Nicomachus, you stay here to guard the place and keep an eye on the mason. And all of you, think about how we're going to get the Scroll back."

"What about the tunnel to the Villa?" asked Grace.

"As long as what the mason says is true, no one even knows about the passage. It's just reconnaissance. Go on. Go! The sooner you go, the more we'll know and we'll have some food too. It must be nearly dusk now."

Nicomachus looked more tired than ever, as if circumstances as well as his age were bearing down on him, but he drew on some reserves of strength. "Harry's is a sensible and brave plan. We'll guard the cavern. I have a weapon here which will protect us if we are attacked."

Once more, Nicomachus reached into his satchel. He drew out a wooden box and opened it. "There are only three of these. One of my colleagues smuggled them out of the armoury before he was taken by Caesar. To be honest, I wanted to dispose of them, but I had no idea how to do so safely. Perhaps they'll be useful after all."

The children gathered round and looked in the box.

"Eggs?" said Grace.

The objects were slightly bigger than ordinary chicken eggs, and coloured light blue with a sort of brown speckle.

"Yes, my children. They are eggs. You throw them,"

Nicomachus said with a smile.

Quintus peered closely at the three eggs, snugly nestled in a little bed of straw in the box. "I hardly think egg on the face of one of Caesar's legionaries is going to stop them for long." He reached out to pick one up, but Nicomachus quickly stopped him.

"Careful! They are very fragile. The yolks are long gone. The contents have been blown out and then filled with Greek Fire. They were part of an experiment in the armoury. I'm told they worked well, but the eggs proved to be far too fragile to be of any practical use. If we ever need these, the impact of the eggs on a hard surface will cause a huge explosion and a fire which no one can extinguish until it burns itself out. You know that only too well, Harry, from your experience in the harbour. Take one of the eggs with you and Quintus, but take care not to crush it. Eleanor and Grace, take another. I will keep one here for protection."

Harry touched the burn on his hand. The burn was healing well, better and more quickly than the memory of the experience. He had no desire to experience that again. "We'll need a sign, then. We don't want to be throwing these eggs at the wrong people."

"I know," said Grace. "The Phoenix. When someone asks you who you are, you give your name and then say "The Phoenix"."

"OK," said Harry, thinking aloud. "Agreed. You say your name and 'The Phoenix.' So you would say 'I'm Grace the Phoenix.'"

"That sounds weird," said Eleanor. "Surely we all know the sound of each other's voices anyway by now."

Grace was thinking too. "No. It's a good idea. It's simple and easy to remember. And also, if we're in trouble and we don't

182

say 'The Phoenix' after our name, you'll know it's us, but that there's danger."

"Good," said Harry. "Let's go then. It's nearly dusk and ideal for Sophie to go hunting whilst you avoid being seen. Quintus, are you ready?"

"Ready as ever, Harry."

32. The City of Rome

Left right. Left right. Left right. The sound of soldiers' feet. The city was full of patrols. Quintus pushed Harry into a low doorway in a side alley. "Hide! I don't know what's going on. I've never seen the city so full of soldiers."

The two of them had found their way into the main sewers, then squeezed up through a drain into the street. Harry was completely disorientated. It was much better on the street, however many soldiers there were. He hated the sewers.

"Now we need to find out what's going on," said Quintus. "Let's hope he's still around."

"Who?" asked Harry, but Quintus didn't answer. They scuttled from here to there, hiding in the shadows and the street corners, dashing from doorway to doorway, avoiding being seen. Then Quintus pushed Harry into another doorway, but this time Quintus tapped on the door sharply, whispering, "Get ready to run if necessary."

"Who's there?" It was another boy's voice. Quintus grinned at Harry.

"Open up, Marcus! It's Quintus."

Bolts squeaked as they were drawn back behind the door. A tiny crack opened. One eye peered through the opening. "Well, well. It's Quintus all right. I thought you were a goner."

"Not me," said Quintus. "I'm a survivor."

"Come in, quickly now. There's a curfew. Why are you risking arrest?"

"What's a curfew?" asked Harry.

"Who's that?" asked the boy, jerking his thumb at Harry.

"This is Harry. He's not from around here."

"I can see that," interrupted Marcus. "Smells like us though."

"He's all right." Harry and Marcus nodded at each other. Marcus carefully bolted the doors and sat down. "Come in. You're welcome - both of you - not that I've much to offer." He put a jug of water and three earthenware cups on the table. "There's some bread left, and I've got some olives."

Harry and Quintus drank gratefully, and pulled off chunks of bread from the loaf. Quintus ate the olives eagerly, but Harry found them too bitter.

"So where've you been?" asked Marcus, when the boys were able to speak.

"Egypt, actually. But that's another story. We're back now and we need your help." Quintus paused and then spoke softly, as if the words were difficult. "I'm in the same boat as you now. No parents."

"I'm sorry," answered Marcus quietly. Then Quintus went on in a more normal voice, "So what's going on? Why the soldiers? Why the curfew?"

"They started it yesterday. No one's allowed on the streets after dark."

"But that's unheard of in Rome! There must be an uproar."

Marcus looked at the other two boys, his eyes turning from one to another. "Don't you know?"

"What?" snapped Quintus.

"You really don't know, do you?"

185

"Know what, for Jupiter's sake!"

"Caesar is virtually at war with the Senate. Rome is awash with rumours. Cicero, the great defender of the Republic, is stirring everyone up against Cleopatra, calling her a vile magician. He says that Cleopatra is the so-called Queen of Kings and Caesar wants to be King of Kings."

Harry wondered whether this would change anything. Or it might not. They still had to contend with Cleopatra and, more to the point, with Neos. They had to recover the Scroll and to ensure Kasya and Hypatia were safe. One thing was certain, Rome would not be an easy place to live in now.

Marcus went on, "Caesar came back to Rome expecting a triumphant welcome. He wasn't given one. Cleopatra has been snubbed and is a virtual prisoner in her villa, while Caesar plays politics. Then there are all the evil omens in the city and the rumours about the magic that Cleopatra has cast over both Caesar and Rome itself."

"But how has this all happened?" asked Quintus, bewildered by this turn of events. "There must be a lot of changes in the city. If there's war between Caesar and the Senate it will affect the whole empire!"

"It's a war of power. Caesar has been called perpetual dictator and claims he has the powers to rule the world."

"What were the omens?" asked Harry, not too interested in hearing about the politics of Rome.

"First, there was the bird that everyone saw high above Caesar's ship when it arrived. The soothsayers said it was the Phoenix. Many doubted it. Then there were the starlings, thousands of them. Probably millions. They swarmed over the soldiers coming from the port and then flew right over the city itself. It was like the Sun had been taken away in the middle of the day."

"I guess they are the ones that freed us," muttered Harry, as Quintus continued.

"And then there's the big cat, as big as a lion, but it wasn't one. I saw it myself on the Capitol. It glared at me and showed its teeth." Marcus shuddered. "They were like daggers. Thank the gods, it passed me by. It's been seen marauding around the city, especially near the Appian Way and Caesar's big villa just there. It's been killing sheep outside the city, but there are people who say it's been killing babies too. There might be more than one, because some reports say it's black, others say it's stripy. One thing's clear. The Senate and the priests of all the temples all say that Cleopatra is a witch and must be deported to Egypt immediately. The Villa Appia where she's staying is so closely guarded nothing can get in or out. They're sending her back to Egypt tomorrow. Even Caesar has agreed."

Harry jumped to his feet. "We need to get going now, then! This is a disaster. Hypatia and Kasya - and Neos - will have to go back with her. They'll be lost, let alone the Scroll and everything else! We need to tell the others as soon as possible. We'll have to do something tonight!"

"How?" said Quintus. "And what?"

It was Marcus's turn to look bewildered. "What are you talking about? You sound as if you know something about all this."

Harry was trying to think. There was an idea bubbling up in his mind, but it wasn't properly formed yet. He got up to pace the tiny room. Three steps across, three back, ignoring Quintus and Marcus for the moment.

Then suddenly the idea resolved itself in his mind. It was crazy, but it might just work.

"Marcus, Quintus. The cat? How would it get in and out of the Villa Appia?"

"If it's in the Villa Appia," said Marcus.

"It is," Harry and Quintus said together. Harry continued, "It's Cleopatra's pet."

"Well," said Marcus, "since the place is so heavily guarded, it must move around like us - in the drains."

"That's what I thought. And how many drains would there be coming from the Villa Appia."

"Well, just one," said Quintus, as if Harry was stupid.

"Good."

"What are you thinking?" Quintus asked.

"We've got to kidnap the cat. Kidnap, not kill. Tonight. Now, actually."

33. Kidnap

Harry's idea was simple enough. The demonic link between Pyrros, the Ptolemaic cat, and both Neos and Cleopatra was so strong, Harry believed they could force a swap between the kidnapped cat and the Alexander Scroll. They should have a chance of rescuing Kasya and Hypatia as well. With the cat kidnapped, they could draw Neos into the cavern and force his hand. That was the idea anyway. If Cleopatra was about to go back to Egypt, now was the time to capture the cat, not later after thinking it through.

Marcus needed no encouragement to join them. He wanted some adventure, he said. Quintus took to it with enthusiasm. "It'll be easy - like catching a rabbit in a net when it pops out of its warren," he said. Harry was not so sure.

First, risking the curfew, Marcus had led them to the back end of the fish market. The whole place was rank with the stink of rotting fish. They had 'borrowed' a strong fishing-net and found some short fish-spears as well. They carried the awkward bundle of the net down the main drain under the Appian Way. Crouching under the low roof, Harry splashed through water and sewage. He tried not to think about what was squelching under his feet and spreading between his toes. Once he trod on something that squealed and nearly tripped him over.

"What was that?" he muttered.

"It's only a rat," answered Quintus. "Harmless."

Harry thought about stories he'd heard of rat bites, plague and so on, but no more rats interfered with their slow progress to the place Marcus and Quintus said was the junction with Villa Appia's drain.

They couldn't know whether the cat would be coming out of the house or returning to it from one of its marauding raids. They laid the net on the ground and got ready to entangle the cat and wrap it up like a parcel as soon as the creature walked across the trap. Marcus had brought a tiny oil-lamp in his pocket.

Now they just had to wait. Sitting in the drain, constant drips of water (or perhaps something more unpleasant), splashed from the ceiling onto Harry's neck, and ran down between the rough gown he had been wearing all this time and the chainmail coat. In the darkness and silence Harry was beginning to have doubts about his plan. Was it a scatterbrained idea? The problems all unravelled themselves in Harry's mind too quickly - and too late.

A splash alerted them. Something was coming up the drain. Could it be the cat? It was pitch black in the drain. Another worry. Or would it help them? The boys would just need to feel a tug on the net. It was more like fishing than hunting rabbits with a net.

The splashing stopped. Harry tried to control his breathing to listen. There was certainly an animal there, but was it the one they wanted? It sniffed the air. It could smell them! What fools they had been, not to think of that! But the net stank of fish. Maybe the smell would cover up the smell of the boys. Now they probably smelt just like the drains anyway.

Was that a tug on the line? Harry tightened his grip. The

animal was on the move. Now there was definitely a tug. The cat was taking it very slowly - wary of the net, probably. If they tried to catch the animal before all four feet were on the net, surely it would escape. But how could they tell how far it had crossed?

More tugs - stronger.

"Now! Now!" he shouted. The boys ran towards each other, bumped into each other in the darkness, and flung the net around whatever it was. The animal was screeching and spitting. It was strong. Harry felt its claws trying to rip him open, but the chain mail protected him. He hung on desperately, hoping Quintus and Marcus could manage the ropes. The screeching continued.

"I think we've - got - it!" gasped Quintus.

"Hold on, I've got a lamp," said Marcus. There was the scrape of tinder and then a tiny light blossomed in Marcus's hand. At their feet lay an untidy bundle containing the Ptolemaic cat, kidnapped, furious and screeching. They wound more ropes around a leg that was poking out of the net, and some rope must have got between its jaws, for it spluttered and the screeching stopped.

"We did it! We did it!" yelled Quintus, dancing up and down with excitement.

"I never thought it would work!" shouted Marcus. "We caught it by ourselves!"

"Sshh! Not so loud!" said Harry, though he too wanted to yell with triumph. "Come on. We've got to get it back to the cavern."

Though it was now late at night, the others were still awake. There was no point even attempting to sleep - they were

191

worrying too much about what might have become of Harry and Quintus. They had eaten some of the game that Sophie had hunted, and fed some to the old mason. Then Grace and Eleanor had argued about when - and whether - they should go and try to find the boys. Finally, it was settled that they would wait until dawn.

Before the boys even reached the cavern they could smell roasting meat. Harry was so hungry that his mouth watered and dribbled on to his chain mail. When they entered the cavern they felt the pleasant warmth of the fire.

The boys dumped the writhing body of the cat on the floor, entirely forgetting to use the password they had agreed. Harry said nonchalantly, "I hope you've left some of that meat for us. We've brought you a present."

Eleanor rushed over to them. "Oh, thank goodness you're safe! We've been so worried!"

Grace and Nicomachus leapt up and followed Eleanor. Grace hugged Harry as hard as she could, and then hugged Quintus. Marcus was standing by, smiling shyly, and it seemed mean to leave him out, so Grace hugged him too. Nicomachus laid his hand on Harry's shoulder and said, "You are safe, thank the gods. But why have you brought us the cat?"

After Marcus had been introduced, Grace and Eleanor were ready to hand round bits of roast rabbit. Quintus and Marcus reached out eagerly for their share, but Harry looked doubtfully at his hands.

"I think I ought to clean up first. My hands are filthy - all over cat and sewage. But what with?"

"It's OK, we've found water not far from the cave," said Eleanor. "Sophie can show you. But hurry up - we want to know what happened!"

Sophie stood up, and stared rather pointedly at Marcus and Quintus, who hastily got to their feet and followed her out with Harry. When they came back and the rabbit had been dealt with, the boys told their tale.

"All we need to do now is some more breaking and entering and another kidnap," said Harry. It was a weak attempt at cheerfulness in the face of the huge task they were setting themselves. The cat was still spluttering with rage and wriggling in its bonds.

"Shouldn't we loosen the ropes a little?" asked Eleanor. "It might be in pain." Sophie sniffed at the net and the beast within it, rapidly turning her nose up at the combination of smells: sewage, stale fish and worst of all, cat.

"Your attitude does you credit," replied Nicomachus, "but this cat is not as pretty as it looks, as I think you know. To loosen its bonds would be to risk its escape and lose our bait for bringing Neos here. We cannot risk it, especially when the boys have already risked so much."

"I suppose you're right," Eleanor sighed. "What are we going to do next?"

They talked about what they were going to do next. The options were limited. In fact, once they realised there was really only one approach, the plan of action was simple enough. They knew they had to use the mason's secret tunnel. But there was so much that could go wrong.

One thing was sure. Time was against them.

34. Challenge

Neos was pacing around his room in the Villa Appia. His anger raged against the whole of Rome, Rome that was keeping him trapped here - under house arrest. And he was angry that his mother was so deeply in Caesar's thrall, especially now that Rome was turning against them.

The cat Pyrros had managed to find a way out of the house but the secret exit and entry through the drain was too small for Neos to follow it, even if he had been willing to go into the sewers.

Neos was also furious that the children and Nicomachus had vanished. He knew that Kasya and Hypatia knew something, but he could not touch them without confessing his own secrets to his mother. Neos did not want to do that. He coveted the power of the Alexander Scroll for himself and feared Cleopatra might give it up to Caesar. His mother was clearly a poor judge of character in admiring Caesar so much. Thinking about her, the Queen of Egypt, being slighted by the Romans made Neos so furious that he couldn't sleep. All he could do was pace up and down in his bedroom late at night, crazy with rage and frustration. And where was that cat anyway? Shouldn't it be back by now?

Back in the cavern, Nicomachus asked the old mason to tell them how to open the secret door into Villa Appia. The man crumpled to the floor, arms around his knees, crying out, "I can't tell you. It's my secret. My secret. They'll kill me if I tell you." All the madness had returned to him.

The children watched impatiently as Nicomachus talked to him, "Don't tell me, then. Open the door for me instead. We don't need to know the secret. Just show us the way."

"There's no way this is going to work," whispered Harry to the others.

But Harry was wrong. Slowly, Nicomachus drew the old man to his feet, "You need not open the door for me. Do it for the children. Show the children."

"For the children?" asked the old man.

"For the children." Nicomachus beckoned Eleanor and Grace and placed the old man's hands in theirs. "Now," he whispered into Eleanor's ear, "before he changes his mind again."

Blind as he was, the mason led them up the passage with confidence, hand in hand with the girls. At the end, he let go of them. He stroked the smooth stone wall with his hands, caressing it like a pet and talking to it. "My best work you are. Now I'm here with you again." His right hand reached out to the side feeling for something, a latch. Then his hand wavered. His legs trembled.

Eleanor saw him hesitate. She took his hand gently. "Please do it for us."

"For the children. Yes. For the children." He pressed something. A sharp click, and the stone door swung smoothly open. But that broke him. He turned and ran down the passage whimpering in fear. Quintus, Marcus and Harry let him pass them without touching him.

"I wish we could come," said Quintus. "I must say, I'd like to see inside the Villa."

"No, you're needed here. Nicomachus isn't strong and he might need help with the old man."

"Where do we look for Kasya and Hypatia?" asked Harry.

"Easy - in the kitchens," said Grace. "They'll be there, or nearby. It's lucky this door leads into them. The old man said he could hear the servants talking."

"No," interrupted Marcus. "You said Hypatia is Cleopatra's personal servant, so she'll be sleeping in the antechamber to one of the big bedrooms. I expect Kasya sleeps with her. You need to go to the garden - the peristylium. All the important rooms open out of there."

"How do you know?" asked Grace. "You haven't been in the Villa."

"All big Roman houses are built the same way," said Marcus. "Just find the peristylium and hope you get the right bedroom. Don't confuse the peristylium with the atrium, though. The atrium's got a pool in it. The peristylium is just a garden."

"Good luck," said Quintus.

Harry thought it would be just their luck if they found Neos's bedroom instead, but he didn't say so.

They crept through the old mason's door into the empty kitchen, and saw another door ahead of them. Harry opened it silently, and they found themselves in a huge hall, floored with marble. The walls were painted with lifelike pictures of Roman men and women, and in front of them was a long rectangular pool.

"The atrium," whispered Eleanor.

"Yes, and look!" whispered Grace, "I can see trees over there! Through that next bit. That must be the peristum."

"Peristylium," whispered Harry. "Come on, then!"

Fortunately it was easy to tell which must be Cleopatra's bedroom because of the strong musky scent which came from it. Sure enough, there was a little room built on to the wall outside. It was barely more than a shed. Grace peeped inside and was deeply thankful to see Kasya and Hypatia asleep on a rough mattress on the floor. While Eleanor and Harry waited nervously outside, Grace gently shook Kasya. She woke, and finding a stranger bending over her, drew breath for a scream. Grace put her hand over Kasya's mouth, nearly screaming herself when Kasya bit her hand. Then they recognised each other. Grace put a finger on her lips to say 'keep quiet', while rubbing the bitten hand against her leg to relieve the pain. Kasya mouthed the words, "I'm sorry." Then, in the quietest of whispers, Grace said, "We've come to free you. We want to bring your mother too. Do you think she'll leave the Queen?"

"Is Nicomachus with you?" asked Kasya.

"Yes, he's waiting for us."

"Then I think she will."

Hypatia woke instantly and much more quietly than Kasya. She refused to leave Cleopatra at first, but Grace said "Nicomachus is waiting for you."

"Mama, if we go with them we'll be free! We'll never have to look at the floor and say 'Yes, Madam' ever again!"

"I wish I knew what to do," sighed Hypatia.

"If you don't come I won't leave you," said Kasya.

"Come with us!" said Harry. "We need you and we can't wait much longer. Listen, this is our plan."

When they had explained the plan to Hypatia, she sighed again. "I will come with you and help where I can. Kasya deserves a chance of freedom and I could never leave her.

Now - Neos's room is the other side of the courtyard. We're in luck. The outside of the house is heavily guarded, but inside are only the household slaves. If we wake them, I'll try to bluff our way through, but everyone is so exhausted, they may not wake."

Eleanor's dagger was at her side. She checked that it would pull smoothly out of its scabbard, though she hoped she wouldn't have to use it. Harry carried some rope to tie up Neos. Grace had a piece of cloth to gag him. They crossed the peristylium to his door without incident, but they could hear him pacing up and down. The children looked at each other in dismay. That wasn't part of the plan! He was meant to be asleep! They waited. Neos must not make a noise when they grabbed him.

Harry made a decision. "Count to five and then come in and help me." Before they could question or stop him, Harry just walked in. He smiled at Neos and put his finger to his lips to tell him to be quiet. It was enough for Neos to break off his pacing and listen.

"I've got something for you, something you want," whispered Harry in a conspiratorial voice. He made it sound like a friend, not an enemy.

It was enough to surprise Neos. He took a step toward Harry and at that moment the others rushed in and thanks to Hypatia's weight and strength, they soon had him overpowered. Grace and Kasya sat on his legs. Harry clamped a hand over his mouth and Eleanor showed him her dagger, glowing green. She whispered fiercely, "One sound and you get this!" She held the dagger against Neos's neck.

"I'm going to gag you," said Harry, 'but as long as you behave you won't get hurt. Now listen. I've got your monstrous cat. You can have it back but we need the Scroll. Bring it and come with us." Neos's eyes lit with the orange fire. Grace was glad that

Harry had gagged him - she was sure he would have cursed and sworn at them otherwise. Neos's eyes darted towards a bag on the table. As he struggled, the point of Eleanor's dagger pushed more firmly against his skin, threatening to draw blood.

"Oh, it's in there is it?" hissed Eleanor. "Well, once we have you nicely tied up, we'll check and then you come with us anyway."

The Scroll was in the bag. Tied up and manhandled by the children and Hypatia, Eleanor's dagger still pricking him, there was nothing Neos could do except glare at them with his fiery eyes.

"Let's go, then," said Harry. "Back to the cavern."

"Phew!" said Eleanor. "We did it! I'm not sure how, though."

"I can never repay you for this night's work," said Hypatia, taking Grace's hand. "To see my daughter a free woman! It's what I have always longed for."

Kasya took Grace's other hand and squeezed it tightly.

But when they left Villa Appia, they never heard a faint scraping sound. The secret stone door had not shut properly behind them. It almost closed, then swung back on its central pivot. The passageway was wide open.

35. Cleopatra's Curse

In the underground cavern, Harry removed the gag from Neos's mouth. Even though he was bound and a prisoner, he bore himself with the haughtiness of his mother. He ignored the children. But his eyes were still filled with orange flame as he looked at the writhing bundle in the net. The demonic cat's struggles ceased and it looked back at its master, its eyes also aflame. There was an understanding between them that made Harry anxious.

Neos spoke to Nicomachus with venom. "You are a traitor to my mother and the Pharaohs of Egypt. Your actions are treason against us and the memory of our dynasty. And you betrayed your promise to help unravel the mysteries of this Scroll. Or perhaps you are not a traitor? Prove it now. Hand back the Scroll and return to Egypt with us. Help me to use its power and you can sit by my side and my mother's as we conquer the world and revenge ourselves against the arrogance of Rome. You shall have all the power you want."

With the Scroll in his hand once more, Nicomachus was relieved and reassured. "I do not seek power and I have never been a traitor. I have kept my oath to Alexander, deservedly known as The Great. He was respected across the world. You seek power for its own sake and that power you will not win.

200

You will never have this Scroll."

"I will have it!" shouted Neos. "It will be mine! Then I alone will command its powers, especially now I have destroyed the other scrolls in the fire in the Library of Alexandria."

"That was you?" asked Nicomachus, astounded at the boy's boast.

"Yes. I did it. Though I didn't even have to ignite the Greek Fire thanks to that foolish soldier who slipped up," replied Neos. "I will take the Scroll now."

Neos's eyes turned back to the cat and Harry saw the slightest of nods. What did it mean? But there was no time to find out. The cat leapt from its bonds in a single move. All its writhing and wriggling had paid off. Its sharp claws had torn through the rope and as it launched itself at Nicomachus, the old librarian moved his hands to his face to protect his eyes, one of which this very cat had taken from him centuries before. This time, however, the cat was not after his eyes. It knocked the Scroll from his hands and twisted in the air towards Neos with a grace that belied its evil character. The Scroll fell onto the floor. With a crack, the wooden end broke. A small crystal vial rolled out and lay at Neos's feet. Neos stared at it. The cat moved behind him and tore with its razor-like teeth at the ropes that bound his hands.

Harry moved towards it, but Nicomachus did not budge. With his hand in the air, he indicated that they should draw back. The cat was a creature that could destroy armies. Harry stopped, but he had no intention of doing nothing. He saw that Neos was mesmerised by the vial, picking up the little object and turning it in his hands. Harry indicated to the other children to move back to the walls of the cavern. He began to creep around the outside of the cavern, slowly edging around the walls, but not before whispering to the others, "Put your fingers in your ears."

"What is this?" said Neos sharply, holding up the vial.

"It is a curse, a poison," replied Nicomachus. "Drink it at your peril."

Neos sneered, "You want me to drink it, do you?"

"Yes, I'd like you to drink it," said Nicomachus calmly. "It will end our troubles and we will be rid of you."

Neos looked sharply at the old man. "You're not the sort to kill a child, the son of The Queen of Kings. I think it's not a poison. I think it's something quite different. And I think you know what it is. It's been hidden in the most sacred of places - in the end of the Scroll. This is the potion that has been rumoured for generations, a potion no one believed existed. This is the gift of immortal life."

"I tell you, it is a curse," Nicomachus answered. "Drink that, even one drop, and you will never be the same. Take the stopper off and smell its foulness. The taste is even worse."

Neos opened up the bottle and instantly the whole room became filled with the foulest of smells, making them all feel sick. He answered angrily, "How do you know about the taste?" He pointed to Eleanor. "I heard you when you had that traitor in your study in the Library. I was listening under the floor. You told her you are over four hundred years old. He's bluffing - I'll prove it!" He lifted the vial and poured the whole contents down his throat. Eleanor put her hands to her mouth to stifle a scream, while Quintus shouted 'No!' Neos tossed the empty bottle on the floor and looked arrogantly at Nicomachus. "See. I'm still alive!"

Grace was nearly in tears. Neos had not only command of the Scroll, but had also drunk the immortality potion. What

202

could they do?

Unnoticed, Harry had reached the back of the cavern. He put his hand into his pocket for the egg full of Greek Fire and pulled it out. He hoped it would work. He put one finger in an ear. "Not enough hands to protect my other ear," he thought to himself. Then, just as he was about to throw the egg down on the ground, Neos put a hand to his throat. His eyes opened wide, staring. He fell to the floor, retching and coughing.

"I told you it was a curse," said Nicomachus.

Harry was confused. What should he do? Nicomachus had told them it was the potion, not a poison. The cat was still just as much of a danger though. At the sight of its master in agony on the floor, it crouched ready to spring, staring at Nicomachus with its orange-flaming eyes, its tail lashing back and forth.

Harry threw the egg down on the ground. There was a blast like a huge thunder flash. Flames spread across the floor. Anyone unprepared would be completely disorientated and deafened, including the cat. This was his moment, while the cat was stunned. Harry felt dizzy from the shock. His uncovered ear was agony, and a trickle of blood dripped down his cheek, but he had been prepared. The cat was shaking its head from side to side, obviously in pain too. Harry reached under his chain mail and pulled out the dragon's claw. Launching himself into a flying tackle, he landed squarely on the cat's back, forcing the dragon's claw, full of venom, into the creature's neck. The cat slumped. Harry slumped on top of it.

Eleanor ran in and held her dagger to the animal, making sure it really had been defeated. Neos's body was now face down on the floor and he had ceased moving. Grace and Kasya tried to help Hypatia, Nicomachus and the old mason, all of whom had been unwarned. They were deaf from the blast, too stunned to move.

The eerie silence that followed the explosion was suddenly torn apart by an agonising scream. Cleopatra appeared in the cavern from nowhere. She threw herself at the body of her son and looked at his eyes, seeing nothing but emptiness in them. She cried the haunting wail of a mother who has lost her child. Then she arose and surveyed the room. Though she was dressed in a plain white night robe, she had never looked so dangerous. Her face was a twisted mask of rage, grief and thwarted power. She wore a cobra around her neck, a living stole, its lidless eyes staring malevolently.

"Who is responsible for this?"

She stood still, waiting for an answer. Her eyes shone as Neos's and the cat's had before, with a vengeful orange fire, the reflection of the evil Nether World and the bond she and her ancestors had made with the demonic cat.

She thrust her arm out at them, pointing. "Who?" The snake slithered down her outstretched arm. The forked tongue darted out above her pointing finger. It was a symbol of her authority.

Harry rose from the cat, sure now that it was dead. Eleanor rose too and Grace moved away from Nicomachus.

Harry said, "We did this. We are protecting the secrets of the Alexander Scroll. It is you, not us who is responsible for your son's death, though. He was the greedy arsonist who destroyed the Library of Alexandria. Your demonic quest to command The Nether World has caused this."

The three children were a contrast to the Queen. Small, scruffy and, in Harry's case, covered in both sewage and blood, they stood firm. Harry continued, "If you had not sought the powers of The Nether World, if you and Caesar had not dabbled in the evils of a realm that humans should not be involved with, none of this would have happened. Your son would not be dead and nor would your evil cat."

"How dare you speak to me like that!" replied the Queen angrily the flames in her eyes so strong that they mimicked the fork of the snake's tongue. "I could destroy you easily - like swatting a fly."

Grace put her hand in her pocket and pulled out her egg full of Greek Fire. She said, astonishing herself, "No, you can't. But I can destroy you with another explosion. And if necessary, I will. Take your son and your cat away with you and return to Egypt, otherwise you will be burnt with the fire you tried to burn Harry with." She was amazed at the forceful way she had spoken. She was far from sure that she could throw the egg at Cleopatra and burn her with the evil fire.

Cleopatra looked at the three children again. The orange fire in her eyes grew deeper and changed to red, the pupil narrowing to the tiniest of pinpricks. "What is your purpose? Are you sent here to hunt me down? Are you demons sent to haunt me? No. I think not. You, in your piteous rags, you are mere mortals who have meddled in things that do not concern you. You have frustrated me for now, but I will be revenged. This is my promise and my curse. Listen well. I curse you now and in the future. You will never be rid of me. I and my descendants will follow you for all time across the world to track you down and destroy you. Your lives will be cursed by fear of my revenge. This is not the end but the beginning."

With astonishing strength, she lifted her son's body from the floor and draped him over her shoulder. With her other hand she seized the cat by the scruff of its neck and dragged it behind her down the passageway towards the Villa Appia. Not once did she look back.

Quintus and Grace followed her and closed the stone door after her. This time they checked it again, but to make doubly certain, Grace threw the egg of Greek Fire from a safe distance. The flash and blast of the fire did far worse damage than in the cavern. The stone door shattered into rubble and the tunnel caved in. Even through the blast, the children could hear the voice of Cleopatra, cursing them once more.

"Can she really do that? Can she really curse us across all time like that?" asked Eleanor, wide-eyed.

"I don't know," muttered Harry. "I really hope not."

36. Guardians of The Scroll

It was two days before the adults' ears stopped ringing from the blasts and they could hear again. The children had unanswered questions but they had to wait. In that time, they made the cavern their home. Quintus and Marcus ran through the sewers and brought supplies from Rome, finding scraps and begging for bread from Marcus's uncle, a baker, and charitable friends.

The boys brought news back from the city. Cleopatra had apparently gone home with some pomp and respect after all. A man called Mark Anthony, one of Caesar's generals who was emerging as an important political force in Rome, had escorted her to her ship. She was granted all the diplomatic status of a Queen, with no outward hint that she had effectively been under house arrest.

There was no news at all about Neos or the events of the previous days from even the most scandalous gossip-mongers in town. Neos had never been seen in public in Rome and Cleopatra had clearly kept this episode quiet so nothing would ever leak out. One or two people noted the absence of her loyal personal slave, Hypatia, but as they said, slaves are bought and sold all the time.

Grace and Kasya continued their close friendship, and with Eleanor and Sophie they hunted for fresh meat. They went up through the tunnel and out into the countryside and again with Sophie's help proved that no one was looking for them and that the cavern appeared still to be completely secret.

Harry felt confused and homesick. So were the girls, but their companionship eased that. Harry was the odd one out and he was lonely. Though he liked Quintus and Marcus, they had each other, and a common background. He was also worried. As soon as Nicomachus could hear well enough Harry approached him, "What I don't understand is how the cat died?"

Nicomachus answered, "It was the venom from the dragon's claw. I saw you stab it into the animal's neck. That is the only way it could have happened."

"Yes," whispered Harry, not wanting the others to overhear at that moment, "but you said that in order to work, the weapon needed to be used by a dragon-slayer."

"But Grace told us all that you were a dragon-slayer," said Nicomachus. "Isn't that true?"

"Not really. I tried to tell you at the time, but we got interrupted. I fought with a dragon last summer, but I never killed one."

"I see. Yet you still used the claw to attack the cat, knowing that it might not work. That was very brave."

"Well, we were a bit desperate," said Harry, not really enjoying the admiration. "But why did it work?"

"I think, Harry, that the answer must be that it didn't work as we thought. I must look at the Alexander Scroll again in case my memory is faulty." Nicomachus drew the Scroll from his satchel, where it had remained since the fight. "Will you fetch me a lamp, please?"

When Harry returned, Nicomachus said, "May I borrow your Babel Charm to read this, please? It's time you rested, anyway. You will not need it tonight and in the morning I think we will need to have a Council."

"And what about Neos? What happened to him?" asked Harry.

"We'll talk tomorrow." Nicomachus was clear that was to be the last word until morning. "The Charm?"

Harry sighed and drew the chain with his Babel Charm over his head. "Of course you can borrow it."

Nicomachus began to unroll the Alexander Scroll to find the right place. He looked up in a kindly way and waved Harry to his sleeping-place.

Knowing he would never sleep until had some answers, Harry settled down on the floor of the cavern, expecting a wakeful night. Because he was so sure he would be awake thinking all night, he was utterly surprised when he had to be shaken awake in the morning. "Harry, wake up," said Eleanor. "Nicomachus wants to gather us together for a Council."

Harry rubbed his eyes, "I know."

"Oh?"

"Yes. We agreed it last night. I hope he's found out the answer."

They sat in a circle, the three children from the future, Nicomachus with a long history going back into the past, the two Roman boys, Kasya, Hypatia and even the old mason, wavering between sanity and madness. As ever, Sophie formed part of the group, watchful, loyal and strong.

After returning the Babel Charm to Harry, Nicomachus began, "Harry has been troubled by something and asked me about it last night."

He nodded to Harry, who said, "I couldn't understand why the cat died. As you girls know, I'm not a dragon-slayer, and

Nicomachus told us ages ago that the cat could only be killed by dragon venom wielded by a dragon-slayer."

"Yes," Nicomachus continued. "That is what the Scroll says. We must therefore assume that the cat is not dead but wounded, and as long as the dragon's claw remains in its body, it will remain unconscious. This means we must be wary in the future. However, this is a relatively small concern for us now compared to the thought that has been worrying me for the last two days."

"What's that?" asked Grace.

"You realise of course that Neos is not dead either."

"But you said it was poison. We saw him drink from the vial. You warned him - " Kasya stopped half way through the sentence. " - and you told us it was the immortality potion as well."

"I know. I hoped he would not drink it and that there would have been some other way out of the problem. The potion was indeed the potion of longevity."

"So why did he die - or appear to die?" asked Grace, also confused by it all.

"I told you that the potion smelt and tasted awful. I did not tell you about its immediate effect. Once taken, it puts the body into a deep coma until its power begins to work on the soul of the person who has drunk it. I was asleep for a week after I had been given it.

"However, I drank only a few drops. Neos took the full bottle. That means the power of the longevity potion may be multiplied by many thousands of years. His initial coma will certainly be deeper and stronger than mine. Neos is not dead. He is immortal and so a danger to us all and to the Scroll in the future. Remember he is not entirely human but also bound into the evils of The Nether World through his connection with the cat, Pyrros.

"We have the Scroll now, along with the Babel Charms and the remaining vial of potion, but be assured Neos will be searching for them throughout eternity to gain power and revenge. This is the result of the curse of Cleopatra. This is my problem."

Nobody spoke, until Eleanor said at last, "It's not your problem. It's our problem. Especially Harry, Grace and me. I don't know why, but it is."

"Eleanor's right," said Grace. "There's something that binds The Palace Library in our time with the Alexander Scroll. There's something the White Phoenix was trying to tell me before this all started. And there's far more that Great Uncle Jasper and Edgar were going to tell us before The Palace Library sent us to you."

"Of course," added Harry. "Time is so confusing, but maybe this is where it starts. This is a beginning of something new. Deep in the past the caretakers of the Alexander Scroll, the Babel Charms and the immortality potion knew these secrets and swore to protect them." He turned to Nicomachus. "Then you and the others in the Library of Alexandria took up the burden. You are the last, but we should be a new start, especially knowing what we do about Neos and the cat. Don't you agree?"

Grace was drawing invisible marks on the floor. "That's right, but I think everyone here should decide who's in or out. Who wants to be a part of this? We're tied up in this somehow, but Kasya and Hypatia and Quintus and Marcus don't have to be. It's not fair on them. If you want out, you should go now."

As she spoke, Grace felt tears run down her cheeks. She was overcome with homesickness. Her only real family were Harry and Eleanor, and this was not their home or time. She loved

Kasya as a friend, but their time together would be short. Kasya held her hand, trying to comfort her. Then there was a voice only Grace could hear - the voice of the Phoenix. "You shall go home very soon. Be patient." That was enough to comfort her. She knew it was true and she stopped crying.

"Well?"

"There's no way you're leaving me out of this," said Quintus. "I'm in."

"Me too," added Marcus.

Kasya paused. "I'm in but I can't leave my mother alone if she doesn't want to be in. She is my only family now."

Hypatia looked at her daughter. "How can I not join you and support you all?"

"But how will you live?" asked Eleanor. "You're escaped slaves. Will they be searching for you? Have you got any money?"

Hypatia smiled. "I doubt the Queen will be searching for us - she is far away by now, and no one else will trouble themselves. Besides, Kasya and I are Greek, not Egyptian. We can pass for Romans. As to what we will do - " her face became sombre, " - I don't know yet, but I am a hard worker and a good cook."

Marcus said, rather red in the face, "My uncle needs help in his bakery. I'm sure he would take you on."

Nicomachus looked at them both. "That would be a good solution for a start. And there is something else you two should know." He said with kind benevolence, "Kasya, I have always wanted to tell you this, but it was too dangerous. Hypatia is not your only family. She is my granddaughter and you are my great-granddaughter. Longevity is in many ways a curse and those few of us who accepted the responsibilities of our role made a decision not to have children, for to outlive your children is not what nature intended, but I fell in love with your great-grandmother, Kasya, and that remained a secret even until now. It is the last of my confessions. If you are determined to be new 'Guardians of The Scroll' then it will be a bond of family and not just promises. Marcus and Quintus have no parents. We will take on that role - perhaps with the help of Marcus's uncle."

Kasya spoke up. "What about Harry, Eleanor and Grace? Why don't you include them?"

"In my heart I do, but now the traumas of the last few days are over, my foresight has returned. As well as reading the Scroll again, I looked into my mirror last night. These three are not from this time and they will return to their own time soon. We must say our farewells."

Grace was still creating invisible doodles on the floor. "It's true, the Phoenix is coming back to guide us. He'll be here any minute. Oh dear, I'm going to cry again. I'll miss you all so much."

Eleanor said, "We need to create a link with you. I've been thinking how and I think we need a symbol that will survive through time and remain secret. I did think the sign of the Phoenix, but that's too complicated. We need something simpler."

"I know!" said Grace. "I've been drawing it on the floor."

"Draw it in the Scroll. I have a brush and ink here in my bag," said Nicomachus.

"Are you sure?" said Grace. She knew not to draw on books, especially valuable books.

"Of course. This Scroll is central to what we are."

So Grace took the brush and the small pot of ink and painted her symbol. It was a square box with a 'V' drawn in the middle.

"Why that?" asked Harry.

"Well the 'V' represents an open book." She turned to the others. "In our time books are lots of sheets of paper bound together, not rolled in scrolls. And the box just tidies it up." She grinned cheekily. "It's easy to do, as well. That way even someone who draws as badly as Harry can do it simply."

"Oi! Don't be rude!"

They all laughed, and then agreed that the pattern Grace had drawn would be the sign of the Guardians.

Then Grace stood up. "The Phoenix is coming. Now. We must hurry." There was the sound of wings and the White Phoenix from the children's time flew in from the tunnel to guide them. Grace said to Harry and Eleanor, "The door into The Palace Library is open again. We haven't much time."

Their goodbyes were unsatisfactory and rushed. They hugged each other. Hypatia tried to wipe the tears from their eyes, ignoring her own. The whole party walked up the tunnel together, guided by the Phoenix ahead.

Then Grace, Harry and Eleanor could see into a corridor full of books, with a dusty leathery smell wafting towards them, the same corridor Grace had walked out of, a week or so before.

"This is it. This is our path," said Grace confidently.

"But that's just the Roman countryside," said Quintus, looking into bright sunshine that also flooded the entrance to the cave. He pointed. "And can't you see the Golden Phoenix flying there?"

"That's truly our gateway back to the Library then," said Harry. He was about to step through, when Eleanor shouted. "Wait! Aren't we being silly about the Scroll? If we take it with us, then it will come 2,000 years into the future and be safe there."

"But will it be safe?" replied Harry. "What about the man

I saw in the night with the fiery eyes, stealing something from the Library?"

"But we'll arrive back after that time, won't we? The Scroll will come home with us," said Eleanor.

"I just don't know," said Harry.

Grace had her eyes on the corridor full of books. The light in the corridor was brightening as if dawn were coming, but unlike dawn nothing was becoming clearer. The books were fading and she thought she could see the sky.

"There's no time to talk about this! We have to go now! The door is closing! Come on!"

Eleanor raised her eyebrows to Nicomachus, silently questioning him. He had kept the Scroll in his satchel around his neck ever since they recovered it. He lifted the strap from his shoulder and handed it to Eleanor. "I think Harry's right. Look after the Scroll. Take it. Farewell."

She took the bag and the three children dashed through the entrance. Running into The Palace Library, the bag caught on something, so Eleanor turned and tugged at it. But it looked as if it was floating in mid-air back in the cave. She saw Nicomachus, Hypatia, Kasya, Marcus and Quintus waving at her. Suddenly they faded and with a snap they disappeared. Eleanor fell over, and looked stupidly at the leather straps in her hand. Detached from the satchel and cut off by the closing gateway, the Scroll remained firmly in the past.

The Palace Library Series

If you enjoyed *Guardians of The Scroll*, be the first
to hear about sequels and new releases!

Ask your parents to sign up to my no-spam mailing list at:

thepalacelibrary.com/gots

The sequel to *Guardians of The Scroll* will be released in 2016.

Read the first chapter on the following pages.

The beginning of the sequel

Nearly 400 Years Later

"I told you the rumours would prove true. There's bound to be gold there. Look! These recent sandstorms have uncovered the tomb."

"But if these rumours are true, so might be the others," grumbled the second man.

"You're not still going on about those old ghost stories are you?" The first man struck his camel impatiently to make it sit. He was dressed in the local Bedouin style with a cloth wrapped around his head and across his mouth to protect him from the frequent sandstorms in the Western Desert.

The other just grunted. They may have been dressed in Bedouin style, but their accents would easily have been identified as foreign, had anyone else been around to hear them. Locals knew better than to come near the place.

The first man was already hobbling his camel whilst the other slid off. Once they were both hobbled with one leg tied underneath them so they couldn't move, the men moved towards the stone obelisk sticking out of the ground, an oddity in the wasteland of endless sand.

"Bring the tools," said the first man, sending the other back to unpack the wrap with the shovels, pickaxes and rope.

It did not take long to dig down to a square base at the foot of the obelisk, which they discovered was the roof of a building, completely covered by sand. There was an inscription carved into the stone, preserved in the dry atmosphere of the desert as if it had been carved the day before.

"What's that say?" said the second man.

"How should I know? I can't read any more than you."

The second man ran his fingers over the symbols. "They're not like those other tombs we got all the gold from. They're a different sort of symbol, more like letters than pictures."

"What does that matter? Shut up and dig. Then we can break in and the gold will be ours before anyone else comes. We're first here. They always buried those Pharaohs with lots of gold. It's easy money."

Breaking through the stone took longer than digging, but they made a hole big enough to slip through. With a rope wrapped around the base of the obelisk, the two men climbed down into the tomb, lighting their way with a rough torch of timber wrapped with rags dipped in tar and set alight.

"Pah!" said the first man, swearing. "It's empty. Someone's been here after all."

"No they haven't," said the second man, looking around. "It's not broken into. It's just plain. There aren't even any pictures painted on the wall like the other Pharaohs' tombs."

The only thing they could see was a large solid stone box with a statue of a dark cat on top of it.

"Well since we're here, we might as well look inside the sarcophagus. Maybe whoever's inside that is covered in gold.

You got those shovels? No?! Well shin back up and find 'em. We can use 'em as crowbars"

When the second man returned, the first said. "Here, help me with this statue."

The two of them picked up the statue of the cat. "This feels like real fur, it does. It gives me the creeps," said the second man. They moved it to the centre of the room, where the sun from above shone upon it. "Look, it's changed colour now. It's got brown and red stripes." The second man pointed at the thing.

"Stop being foolish. Next thing you'll be saying is it's come to life. It's just the light shining on it. Give me a hand with this lid."

They used the shovels to open up the stone sarcophagus and as it lifted, it slipped onto the floor and cracked. The men were thieves, not archaeologists. They didn't care. "Look at that. It's just a lead box. I don't know why we bother. Well, I'll just check inside anyway."

The second man went back to have a look at the statue again. This time he noticed there was a chain around its neck attached to something. The chain was gold. There was no honour between these two thieves. He had a look up at the first man, who was busy with the lead box. He kept his back him, to hide what he was doing. Then he whipped the chain from around the cat's neck. Something was stuck into the statue itself, in the animal's neck. It looked like an ornate pendant, so he gave it a good tug and it popped out. At the end was a wrinkly claw of some sort. It looked a bit like a finger, "Yuk," thought the man to himself, "but at least there's some precious metal in this."

He popped the chain over his head and hid it beneath his clothes, just as the first man said, "It's just a body in the lead box, not even mummified, all skin and bones. Just a boy at that.

Very well preserved, though he could do with a haircut."

The second man wasn't listening. He was staring at the cat, It was moving and stretching it's legs as if it had just woken up. The man was frozen to the spot. "It has come alive. It really has," he whispered.

"What's that?" said the first man.

"It's alive, run for it!" The second man climbed the rope as quickly as he could, thinking only of himself.

The first man couldn't speak though. A skinny hand had just reached up from the body in the lead casket and held him firmly by the neck, squeezing on his windpipe. The eyes of the body opened. These were not the eyes of a dead boy. Nor were they the eyes of a living boy. The pupils were pin-shaped and there was an orange flame within them, burning fiercely.

A loud, satisfied purr from the cat filled the room and as it did so, the man in the coffin sat up, keeping a tight grip on the other's throat. "Thank you for releasing me. Your reward is your freedom. But go now, for we are hungry."

He needed no encouragement. As he legged up the rope, he saw the elegant head of the cat change as it opened its jaw and two long sabre teeth shot out to reach for his leg. Reaching the sunlight, he unhobbled his camel and raced towards the horizon.

Inside the tomb, the boy patted the cat like an old friend reunited. The boy's hair reached all down his back. He put the cat onto his shoulders, its legs draped over his chest and climbed up to the roof and the desert, blinking in the sunlight, the first he had seen for over seven hundred years.

The boy saw the inscription at the foot of the obelisk. Unlike the thieves, he could easily read the words carved there and laughed.

"Here Lies the Eternal Resting Place of Ptolemy Neos Philometor."

Ptolemy Neos Philometor began to walk across the desert with the cat. He revelled in his freedom and nurtured his anger against the world.

"Not quite so eternal, Pyrros. But now I think we have had enough sleep. It's time to know the world again."

The Palace Library Series

If you enjoyed Guardians of The Scroll, be the first
to hear about sequels and new releases!

Ask your parents to sign up to my no-spam mailing list at:

thepalacelibrary.com/gots

I love meeting people who enjoy reading my books. If you
want me to visit your school, book club or any other event,
parents and teachers can contact me on

office@stevenloveridge.com

All the best!

Steven Loveridge